Permanence

Sophie Mackintosh is the author of four critically acclaimed novels: *The Water Cure, Blue Ticket, Cursed Bread* and *Permanence*. She has been longlisted for the Man Booker Prize and the Women's Prize; has won a Betty Trask Award; and in 2023 was selected as one of Granta's Best Young British Novelists of the decade. Her work has appeared in *Granta*, the *White Review* and *Tank* magazine, among other publications. She lives in London.

BY THE SAME AUTHOR

The Water Cure
Blue Ticket
Cursed Bread

Permanence

SOPHIE MACKINTOSH

HAMISH HAMILTON
an imprint of
PENGUIN BOOKS

HAMISH HAMILTON

UK | USA | Canada | Ireland | Australia
India | New Zealand | South Africa

Hamish Hamilton is part of the Penguin Random House group of companies whose addresses can be found at global.penguinrandomhouse.com.

Penguin Random House UK,
One Embassy Gardens, 8 Viaduct Gardens, London SW11 7BW

penguin.co.uk

First published 2026
002

Copyright © Sophie Mackintosh, 2026

The moral right of the author has been asserted

Epigraph from *Near to the Wild Heart* by Clarice Lispector, published by Penguin Classics. Copyright © The Heirs of Clarice Lispector, 1943. Translation copyright © Alison Entrekin, 2012. Reprinted by permission of Penguin Books Limited

No part of this book may be used or reproduced in any manner for the purpose of training artificial intelligence technologies or systems. In accordance with Article 4(3) of the DSM Directive 2019/790, Penguin Random House expressly reserves this work from the text and data mining exception

Typeset by Six Red Marbles UK, Thetford, Norfolk
Printed and bound in Great Britain by Clays Ltd, Elcograf S.p.A.

The authorized representative in the EEA is Penguin Random House Ireland, Morrison Chambers, 32 Nassau Street, Dublin D02 YH68

A CIP catalogue record for this book is available from the British Library

HARDBACK ISBN: 978–0–241–77630–8
TRADE PAPERBACK ISBN: 978–0–241–77631–5

Penguin Random House is committed to a sustainable future for our business, our readers and our planet. This book is made from Forest Stewardship Council® certified paper.

Inside each of them, knowledge never scrutinized by others was piling up.

Clarice Lispector, *Near to the Wild Heart*

The Holiday

There had been many hotel rooms for the adulterers, currently peacefully asleep in a large white bed. Enough to qualify them as experts, connoisseurs. Some of these rooms had been modern, with contours hard-planed and sterile. Others were tired or even sordid, designed not for trysts but for airport stopovers, to grant a portion of hurried, adequate sleep. Most often they were luxurious or something close, rooms of starched sheets and creamy stationery and tiny shampoos. And so while Clara didn't recognize the room when they woke up, or, in fact, possess any recollection of the day before, she was not overly surprised to open her eyes and see Francis there, asleep on the unfamiliar pillow next to hers. She blinked. She said his name out loud. He remained asleep, as if drugged.

She observed him in the lucid morning light, noting how he slept with one arm flung above his head and how his chest – finely muscled, scattered with dark, silvering hair – moved with his breathing. She registered the line of his cheekbone, the hollow of his throat, the fringe of his eyelashes against his skin. The longer she looked, the more awed she felt, and the more removed, as if she were a scientist and he under her microscope, wondrous and strange and newly discovered.

Her attention moved to the room itself. Yes, it was a hotel bed, unmistakably, with pristine sheets and a blue velvet throw rumpled at its foot. A polished cabinet next to the bed, clear of any objects. Parquet floor, French windows opening on to a narrow iron balcony, framed by gauzy curtains. She recognized these things, dimly, but could not place them. There was no minibar, no telephone on which to call for room service.

Clara got up and walked towards the first of two white doors, opened it to discover a second room. No bed in this one. Instead her gaze landed on a small blue velvet sofa facing shelves that sat empty except for two books. A novel she and Francis loved, and a study on Flemish still lifes, both bound in red cloth. She hesitated before reaching for the novel, flicking through its pages, putting it back. It was the same edition as her own. Turning round she noted a kitchenette with wooden counters set across the opposite wall, and another window through which she could see building facades, stucco with red carnations crowding their own iron balconies.

She opened all the cupboards and drawers, found a battered pot identical to the one she had at home, and started to make coffee on the hotplate. Slower than usual, she became so absorbed in the task that, for a moment, she forgot that Francis was there. When she remembered he was only metres away, it was a delicious physical blow – the air knocked right out of her.

She had never woken up next to him before.

A tiny white cup she had just taken from the cupboard slipped from her hold and shattered on the floor. She froze. Something was returning to her.

She heard his movements in the bedroom. As she knelt to gather the pieces of cup, she felt a startling panic.

Francis, she whispered.

He was there in the doorway then, his face pale. He recoiled to see her. He held out his hands.

Clara and Francis faced each other as if duelling. A faint breeze came through the window over the sink, slightly ajar, carrying with it the sounds of a city waking up.

They went back to bed. It seemed, instinctively, the only thing to do. Clara had spent their relationship loving Francis mostly in absence, and yet she believed in the body as the truest site of proof. How sweet it felt to touch his skin, even in her disorientation, knowing it like a map. The relief in thinking only of the immediate, the physical, letting everything else recede.

Afterwards they discovered their favourite clothes in the wardrobe. Clara opened the bedroom's second door to find a bathroom, a cast-iron tub with her usual shampoo waiting beside it, next to the jasmine-scented soap that Francis favoured. A sprightly fern. Don't think about it, she told herself. Don't look too closely. Francis frowned but did not say anything. He was very quiet.

They washed and dressed in the clothes that were there for them. They paced the rooms together. Discovering another door, Francis opened it with some trepidation to find a vaulting, deserted stairwell of limewash and marble. He closed it.

Scared to be seen with me? Clara asked, lightly.

Francis shook himself almost imperceptibly. Sorry, he

said. He took her hand as if in consolation, though only for a moment. Together they walked out of the apartment, walked down the old-fashioned, slippery steps one by one. Their footsteps seemed impossibly loud.

Out on the sunny street, bewildered, they started to walk. They seemed to be in a residential area, the street lined with tall, grand buildings, each one the same as the last. Turning a corner, they found themselves in a square of restaurants and bars, cobbled, with a white stone fountain at its centre.

Here they saw other people for the first time: people strolling across the cobbles, people sitting outside at cafe tables, relaxed and happy. The light was golden. The sky was uncannily blue. Violin music swooped through the air. Francis walked quickly through the square, turning off into a side street, Clara lagging behind and enraptured by everything she saw.

Look, she exclaimed as they passed a stall selling mysterious fried things inside paper cones, and one of the two smiling men behind the fryer passed a cone to her without asking for money, without asking for anything. They sat together on a step and ate, suddenly ravenous, what turned out to be salty parcels of courgette flower. A spot of grease on Clara's summer dress, white cotton tied at the waist. It was warm. Francis kissed her on the cheek with a faintly oily mouth and she laughed in relief and scrubbed at her face with her hand, and then kissed him properly to let him know that she didn't mean it. She was dreaming, she thought, or perhaps she was dead, and so in heaven. The happy, brightly dressed crowds moved past them, the buildings old, narrow, with people looking down and smiling at them, waving to each other. She dug her nails hard into her palms, then stopped at once in the fear that she would wake herself up. They carried on walking, discovering a pair of young women playing violins, sentimental love songs that Clara recognized but couldn't name. When Francis reached his hand into his pocket he found unfamiliar gold coins, and he dropped one into their open instrument case.

They walked for an hour, perhaps, until, on turning a corner, they found themselves back in the first square, the one with the fountain. It appeared that the city was a small one, after all.

Let's get a coffee, suggested Clara.

Francis nodded. Sunlight sheened off the white parasols and the checked cloth covering the table they chose.

A red-haired woman was crying at the next table, her fingers at her temples. Clara was amazed at how freely she did it, the uncomprehending sobs of a child. The woman sitting opposite her – small, mouse-like, dressed in green – seemed helpless, but then she started to distract the crying woman by building a fragile tower of sugar cubes. Look! she ordered, over the crying. The red-haired woman lowered her hands, cheeks tear-stained, watching its careful construction. Soon the tower fell in a graceful, brittle arc. At this, both women started laughing. The cubes were all over the table, all over the floor.

Clara looked and looked, fascinated, her eyes darting from one thing to another. A couple sitting on the edge of the fountain and splashing each other. Another couple with armfuls of roses, walking around the square and offering them out, petals falling behind them. Everybody was paired up, she realized. Two by two.

Nobody's here alone, Clara said, gesturing at the people surrounding them. Everyone's in a couple.

Francis craned around. Not everyone, surely, he protested,

surveying the scene for himself. She took a brown sugar cube and crunched it quickly between her teeth. When Francis finally turned back, he stared at her as though he had never seen her before in his life. Taking up his hand, worn from activities she hadn't witnessed, she kissed it, quickly, bashfully. It was heavy. She did not let go.

Where are we? Francis asked.

I don't know, she said. But I have the feeling that it's all right not to know. That everything is fine, and will continue to be fine. Don't you feel it?

It was true, Clara felt this very strongly, though she knew nothing else; that they were safe and well and there was no need to worry about anything any more, that nothing could touch them or discover them or steal them away. The warm air on her skin felt wonderful. Francis didn't answer her. She held his hand tighter. She was hurting him, but he didn't mind. If anything, the discomfort was grounding. This world was vibrantly physical. His cappuccino was hot, the best coffee he had ever tasted. He could still feel Clara's lips against his skin from earlier, pleasure's echo shimmering through his nerves.

When she went to the bathroom Francis checked his wallet surreptitiously. It was his usual one, but the photographs he kept of his wife and daughter were not there, only more of the heavy gold coins. He patted down every pocket of his jacket and trousers, remembering he owned such a thing as a *phone* – a sudden thought, like waking from sleep – and was irritated, puzzled, to discover that was gone too.

On the table next to them someone had left behind a slim newspaper, bearing the headline *True Love Persists!* over a photo of a square crowded with couples. Francis flicked through its pages, but it seemed to contain nothing but romantic poems. It didn't even give the date. He abandoned it.

I'm sorry if this is a strange question, but where are we? he asked the tall waiter who came to take their order. But he only looked at Francis and shrugged.

Clara was right: it was a city of couples. Some old, some young, some well matched and some ill matched, some monogamous, some less so, some ecstatic, some desperately unhappy, some pale and drawn, some who had been there a long time and some who were new. Couples eating and cooking and fucking and arguing and sleeping and dancing and fighting and swimming and drinking and reading, sitting and lying sprawled on floors and sofas and soft surfaces, couples at each other's knees, at each other's throats, hair pooling on laps and pillows, couples with eyes wide and eyes tearful and eyes shut.

In the city there was time for all of this, and more. Time for the ordinary, to which we normally give little value: the arm snaked around the waist as the other cooks, the choreography of vegetables chopped, the name called from another room (*Francis, could you come here a second*, Clara had always dreamed of calling), the magazine picked up and flicked through and discarded on a table, the crumbs in the toaster, the kiss on the side of the mouth, the coffee made and brought to bed.

Time for life beyond the domestic too. Life beyond the internal and the accumulated and protected, life which did not need to be contained. The couples could do anything and could go anywhere they wanted, within the city's limits. It was the only place they could do so.

It was in the third bar that the panic really set in.

Perhaps it had started with Clara calling the apartment *home* as they drank a short and syrupy cocktail of gin and vermouth on an olive-green vinyl banquette seat, surrounded by mirrors, the windows open so the summer air could come in. *Let's go home after this*, was what she had said, and perhaps it had not been in the words themselves but in how Francis had seemed startled in response.

Or perhaps it had been when Clara was washing her hands in the bathroom of that bar, after Francis had been startled and she had excused herself to smooth over the moment, and standing at the basin she'd felt a giddying sense of unreality. And yet those were her hands moving against each other, weren't they? Her nails, unpolished but clean? She'd blinked like a strobe and her hands were still her hands, and the world was still the new world, and the water was hot and plentiful. She was fairly drunk. Love songs played over the sound system, at a tasteful volume. Marble sink, clean white towels. Very nice, all very nice, she said out loud to herself. Walking back to their table, she passed a framed print of a painting called *Still Life with Cherries and Mouse*. It was not a famous painting, but it was a painting that Clara knew, a painting that meant a great deal to her. She paused to observe the pewter jug, the arrangement of food, the lit candle, the mouse as it surveyed the scene. The surprise made her feet hesitate for a second, as if she had forgotten how to take a step. Perhaps it had been that.

Perhaps it had been as they stood in a crowd waiting to cross the road afterwards, the light about to turn, and she had felt them only two insignificant bodies amidst the warmth of so many others, jostling for space like a flock of birds. Perhaps it had been in the unnatural transition of the sunset, the unmoving sky suddenly tinted with peach, and then inky, uniform blue. Perhaps it had been the fleeting sight of another person crying, a man this time, talking passionately through his tears as he sat on a bench with a much younger woman, and how they had not been able to hear what he was saying but they had not really needed to. Perhaps it had been that.

And then they were running. In the wake of the sunset's decisiveness was an eerie twilight, everything close-focus and remote. Couples thronged the streets and squares, hand in hand. They looked at Clara and Francis speeding past, and then looked back to each other, uninterested.

Running into quieter streets then, past trees gently shedding their leaves, past the windows casting pockets of warmth into the night. As they moved further from the centre of the city, they reached residential streets like their own. Their breath came jagged and confused and they were forced to stop for a moment, at the side of the road, dropping to the pavement to rest. A spill of laughter as a door opened and several people streamed out of the building behind them, heading for the city centre that they had so recently vacated. They ignored Francis and Clara. Francis waited until they had left and then stood up, pulled Clara to her feet and started moving again, not running this time but walking with grim determination.

The street lights flickered on. The ground had changed without them noticing, no longer paved or cobbled but now bare earth, reddish under their feet, which sent up a fine dust. Then they turned a corner and there were no more buildings. The red earth darkened as it stretched into the emptiness, seemed scorched, sandy, like the aftermath of a volcanic eruption. They emerged into this void slowly. There was only the dark ground, the darkened sky, and then a slick ring of water, as far as the eye could see.

Francis knelt down, sifted a handful of sooty gravel through his fingers. From this shore they looked back to the city, now haloed with light. The air itself seemed thinner in their lungs. Clara shifted from foot to foot.

They walked back, back towards the centre of the city, and it was even busier than before, almost as if it was a holiday night, with music spilling loudly from the bars and mingling with the sound of buskers stationed on every street corner, photogenic pairs holding electric guitars and microphones, everyone smiling and shining and in their best clothes. Clara and Francis passed the commotion without pausing, crossed the square in which they had had coffee earlier, walked right past the apartment where they had woken that morning, and carried on going until the streets were quiet. But before long there was reddish sand underfoot once more and then the water, the darkness overhead punctuated by a fat pink moon this time, a few gilded stars.

There was nothing to do but return to where they had started the day. Francis was silent. Clara found herself smiling as they moved back from the burnt earth and towards recognizable life, towards the building she was already thinking of as *home*.

Don't think Clara foolish. Single-minded in her devotion, maybe. Committed to the cause of love as organizing principle. And it's not like any of it was so simple.

Which is to say: they tried to leave on the first night, but there was nowhere else to go.

Eighteen months before, in a different city, Clara entered a museum. Outside, humid summer rain. A damp lock of hair across her cheek like a wound. She barely registered the wet of her shoes. The guard watched her, as if she could be unpredictable.

The museum contained a painting from the seventeenth century by an anonymous artist: *Still Life with Cherries and Mouse*. Dark oils, drapery, gilded frame. An artichoke, split into two, on a shining plate. Apples, butter, bread. A knife, a pewter jug to match the plate, a lit candle, the flame caught mid-waver. In the foreground, almonds scattered precisely on the linen covering the table. And the cherries, of course, glossy and ripe and clearly delineated, a dream-cherry, or maybe just how cherries used to be. There was nobody in the painting, only the mouse in the left-hand corner, very alive, intent on the food.

Clara looked at this painting for a long time.

Standing there, she slowly became aware of the presence of a man, a shadow in the corner of her right eye. She turned her face towards him, gradually, and then she was looking at him and he was looking at her, and neither looked away. A fullness grew inside her, which she only vaguely recognized as desire. He was the one to look away first, abruptly moving into a different room. Barely conscious of her feet moving across the parquet, she followed him.

As she entered the next room she took in his dark trousers, white shirt, black curls touched with silver. He seemed *well made*, she thought. He seemed formed with intention, put together, in a way she was not. The paintings glowed inside their lavish framing, but she no longer saw them, his presence absorbing her whole focus. Separated by a glass cube housing an ornate, glimmering porcelain vase, their eyes met again. He moved with a practised, easy grace. Her summer dress of faded floral cotton was belted in the middle, ripped at the hem, and she was free, she felt it but did not fully grasp it, did not understand that there were endless possibilities still open to her.

He walked straight towards her then, and it seemed like he would brush past her, that he would touch her, take her hand, but at the last minute he swerved and she could only sense the heat of his skin, his cologne.

The guards continued to watch them.

She turned around and left the room, an experiment to see if he would follow, did not dare to look. Hot knife of breath, light-headed. He followed her into the next room. He overtook her, and then she followed.

Past her, in a stairwell, sheltered from eyes, he waited. He took her wrist. She stepped closer to him. His other hand drifted to her hair, still wet, then to her cheek. She felt the cool metal of a wedding band.

Her nails were dirty, she was exultant, on the edge of something. She ran headlong towards what felt like the rest of her life.

For a long time she would want to return to the calm of that first room, before anything unforgivable had taken place. When he was just another beautiful and mysterious object, standing still, watching her from a distance.

When Clara woke up the next morning she lay there for a moment, scared to open her eyes. When at last she did, she saw the apartment of the previous day waiting for her. A cold rush of relief left her boneless. She exhaled a long and tremulous breath. Francis was sprawled on his stomach, dead to the world.

She rose and pulled a familiar green linen dress from the wardrobe. In the kitchenette she paused to drink a long glass of water. *Their* kitchen: a shock like touching a tiny exposed wire. Outside, the gradient of the sky was fresh with newly stopped rain. All the windows in the buildings across the road were dark.

She slipped on her sandals and opened the door of the apartment, went down the marble staircase. Outside, she looked up at the tall stucco buildings; the blue-painted wooden shutters, the identical window boxes. There was no movement behind any of the windows. The street turned sharply at the end, where it opened on to another, wider street – she remembered this from yesterday – and then it led on to a network of alleys, washing hung out on lines over the balconies. It was completely empty. The sky was steadily brightening to pale blue, as if a dial were being turned. She faltered, looked back up to where she thought their own window might be.

But Francis would be fine if he woke to find her gone, she reasoned, for he liked the way she was good at being alone, able to occupy herself like a precocious child left to their own devices. It was a necessary skill.

She walked down the street, feeling a new sensation in her chest: a sense of tugging, a formless and uneasy nausea that increased with each step. When she put out a hand to a nearby building, steadying herself, her fingers came back dusted in fine white chalk.

I should go home, she told herself, though she had not walked that far. As she retraced her steps, the sensation in her chest eased. By the time she opened the door to the apartment, it had gone, replaced by joy. Her heart was a lifted sheet, billowing.

Home. How easily the word came to her.

Francis was still asleep. She was delighted by the discovery that he snored, gently. On a wooden chair he had draped his jumper from the day before, a loose navy wool. She lifted it to her face and breathed deeply, reverently, before folding it up and placing it back on the chair.

To have wanted for so long, and then to have. To ask and to receive in attendant simplicity. To have existed mainly within absence and then to have the abundance of *here*: a word so assured, both statement and answer. There was no measuring Clara's gratefulness.

For the entirety of their relationship had been so carefully contained, its boundary lines tight and pristine. There was something incredibly precious about this, they had always believed: to be living inside an uncompromised secret. An ecosystem of foliage and fauna that belonged only to them.

Sometimes the despicable sentimentalities that sustained this love made Clara feel sick. She could not ask if they made Francis feel sick too, out of respect for the ecosystem. Rather she tended to its soil unobtrusively. It was important that he feel very sure that everything they did was beautiful.

Later that day Francis suggested they try another route through the city, another attempt to put the pieces together. And so they went out again, taking their time and pausing at each turning, keeping track of their route. Francis looked up at the sky, which did not change; he examined closely the clusters of small purple or blue flowers that grew in the crumbling mortar of the older buildings, slim-leaved. They reached another warren of winding streets and followed them until they emerged at the foot of a large hill to the east of the city. They walked up roughly hewn steps. A cable car glided overhead. Set into the hill were paths and many ruins, sheltered by green things. Part of the hill was covered in apple trees. Other couples sat on blankets beneath them. Francis picked an apple, held it out for Clara to bite. It was strangely tasteless, dry of juice. They sat down on the grass. The sun grew high, and very hot. Clara found a pebble in the grass, perfectly smooth, and slipped it into her pocket, where it clinked against something metal. She withdrew a gold coin with only mild surprise.

What's the last thing you remember, before here? Francis asked Clara. He looked at her closely.

Clara could remember the lift of a hotel, watching her reflection with unease. Then, abrupt as a scene cut, darkness; then the waking up in the shifting light of the new apartment.

We were in a hotel, she told him. I was on my way up to meet you.

You don't remember a journey to get here? he asked.

I don't, Clara said.

Can you try harder? Francis pressed.

Clara shut her eyes and tried to focus on the sheet of darkness that separated now from before. As she did, the tug of nausea returned.

It makes me feel strange to think about, she said, opening her eyes. She lay back on the grass.

Yes, me too, Francis said, leaning closer to her, kissing her on the forehead. Sorry. I'm just confused.

Me too, said Clara.

It's just — he hesitated — you don't seem troubled by any of this. I wondered if you knew more.

Clara looked up at the sky.

I don't know anything, she said. Not a thing. Maybe it hasn't sunk in. But I'm happy to be with you. I don't want to escape, or wake up, or interrupt whatever is going on. So maybe I also don't want to think about it too hard.

But we must think about it, he said. He was not ungentle.

She took his hand and held it above her, against the sky's bright light. The gold band on his finger glimmered.

Perhaps we are dreaming, he suggested. An elaborate, beautiful dream.

I've dreamed about you often, said Clara, releasing his hand. It's not like this.

That's sweet, he said. I never remember mine.

So, not dreaming. What are our other options? she asked.

A pause.

We're hallucinating, Francis said. Or we're dead.

Both good suggestions, replied Clara.

Would death be like this? he asked.

I would hope so, she said. But I don't know that we've done anything to deserve such a paradise. Or at least, I know I definitely haven't.

Francis smiled, a small, non-committal smile.

Clara felt the disorientation and the happiness wash over her again. She closed her eyes.

I'm glad to be here, she said. Wherever we are.

I'm glad too, he said. But then he sat up and looked out over the vista of the city.

It can't be real, he said.

Does that matter?

Francis looked back at her, nonplussed.

Of course it matters, he said, his voice rising. We're in a city neither of us recognizes, with no idea how we got here, and no way of getting home. We're surrounded by water, and among strangers. Don't you understand?

Home, Clara thought absent-mindedly. Her arm reached out and she took hold of his wrist.

You feel real, she said. You're solid. I can feel your pulse.

They were quiet then. They looked down on the strange place, watching the people moving through its streets, the distant traffic. The edge of the city was clearly visible, the ring of water framing the landscape. In the afternoon light, even the scorched earth looked beautiful.

Clara fell asleep there, in the sun. She was tired from the transit between worlds, perhaps, she thought as she drifted off. When she woke they walked down the other side of the hill, right to its foot, where a bridge of pale stone stretched across a river. They stood on the bridge for some time, among other couples also watching the water, resting. The water ribboned back towards the centre of the city, and they followed it for a while. There were no birds on the river, or in the sky.

Suddenly Francis cried out, dashing ahead and turning off the river path towards the main road, almost disappearing from sight. As Clara broke into a run after him, she felt an echo of the tugging feeling from that morning.

What is it? Francis, wait!

He had stopped at the corner of the main road and was standing in front of a metro station. The sign read *City West*.

There should be information here, he said, turning around to Clara. Something that tells us where we are.

They went down the steps and into the station, but found no ticket machines or maps, and nobody official to ask – only artificial yellow light, and the walls tiled in a dirty chequerboard pattern of red and cream. Two attractive young men sat on a metal bench painted in flaking orange paint, waiting, holding hands.

Apparently not, said Francis, resigned, as they climbed back up to street level.

Clara let him steer her along the street, his hand firm on her back.

We haven't eaten all day. Are you hungry? He paused in front of a grocer's shop, the frontage painted dark green. The question seemed absurd but she realized that yes, she was.

Let's get some supplies, he said.

Francis roamed the cool aisles, examining the packets of dried pasta, the jars of mustard and bottles of wine, as Clara placed ripe peaches in a brown paper bag. She moved slowly, deliberately, feeling the heft of each one in her palm. Their blushing smell rose up. A bottle of wine, a loaf of bread. She paid in gold.

We should go back, she said, once they were outside. She was careful not to say *home*.

As they walked back, they passed an old-fashioned photo booth. Clara's feet slowed. She looked at Francis. A souvenir? she suggested, expecting him to say no, but there was only the tiniest pause before he nodded. He owed her, she thought, as she pushed the booth's curtain to one side.

Clara on Francis's lap, his arms tight around her. His build elegant, coiled tight like a dancer, his skin hot and coursing with blood. Beneath the line of his shirt collar the skin paled abruptly. They kissed and blinked for the camera. When they emerged, a cheerful blonde couple were waiting and everyone smiled at each other. The strip of photos, when it dropped from the slot, was perfect. Mouth on mouth, mouth on neck, eyes on each other, eyes – finally – on the camera.

Our first photos together, Francis said, examining them.

Big moment, said Clara.

A long time coming, Francis said, and then he looked at her with such unexpected softness that she could hardly bear it.

When they returned to their apartment, Francis paused in the living room. He looked at the clothes they had left draped over chairs, the dirty glasses in the sink. He took the photographs from his pocket and studied them again for a moment, before putting them down. Clara held her breath as he turned to face her.

Clara, he said, as if he were trying out her name for the first time. Whatever this place is, we're here together. I don't understand how, but perhaps it doesn't matter.

A smile split across his face, slowly. He reached out to her – boyish, jubilant.

It's what we've always wanted, isn't it? he said. Let's not question it.

Clara nodded. He reached out to her, and they kissed. Clara pulled his T-shirt up, then over his head, and they fell to their knees, and then to the floor. Her hands clasped his strong shoulders – *beautiful shoulders, beloved shoulders*, she thought reverently – his hands were on her face, in her hair, and their mouths were open, and she felt her whole body unfolding to him, his skin sweet against her skin.

Afterwards, naked and content, Clara poured them each a glass of the wine they had bought. They sat on the velvet sofa, leaning against each other. The hazy afternoon light came through the window, curtains open all the way. The photograph strip lay on the table, along with the pebble she had found on the hill. Their bare legs were entwined, stretched out. There was wine in their glasses, there was fruit they had chosen and purchased in a paper bag left on the counter, and this could be the start of a life of shared objects, of shared endeavour. This, Clara thought, could finally be a kind of proof.

In their normal lives Clara could not leave him with anything that would arouse suspicion, so they had grown to stake much on what she thought of as votive objects.

Every time she took a flight she visited the duty-free perfume counters at the airport to spray his cologne on to small cardboard tabs, the same one he had worn in the museum the first day they met. She kept them in her pockets, so that her hands and clothes would bear the scent of him. The woman at the counter smiling and asking, *For your boyfriend?* Yes, she said every time, picturing her apartment with Francis in it rather than her best friend Arturo, waiting for her return. Wheeling her suitcase through the door, calling out in greeting as he came to meet her in the hallway.

A slim charcoal pencil, brought back for her by Francis from a work trip to Paris. But when she suggested she draw him, he skittered away. Too much proof, even if abstract, even if faceless and just the long lines of his body; *beautiful body*, she thought, *beloved body*. He did not even pretend it was embarrassment.

A button from her dress, unremarkable, slightly larger than a penny and black, subtly pearlescent. This one felt risky. But she had argued her case for him keeping it, and won; he could say he had found it in the street, or in the pocket of a jacket, something from a long time ago, something misplaced at the dry-cleaner's. A button was a button, and only he would know that it was a button that had touched her skin, a button unbuttoned by his fingers, pulled by those same fingers from the dress itself in impatience.

Most precious of all was a key card from an early hotel day, kept at the bottom of Clara's bedside drawer. Francis didn't know she still had it. She would turn it over and over in her hands, attempting to summon the room, attempting to summon the feeling. She would do anything to return, she felt sometimes, when she held the lifeless oblong in her hands. It gave no clue to what had taken place in that room, a room where everything had been permitted. The world outside that room had temporarily ceased to exist. The room number was still scrawled on it, and the number itself, over time, started to take on a votive quality too. *501*, Clara would whisper to herself. It was a code, an incantation, a reminder. It was just the number of a room.

That evening they dressed for dinner. In the wardrobe Clara found a pale blue silk dress identical to the one she had been coveting for weeks but hadn't yet bought, thin-strapped and long. The material fell over her body like water. She was on edge as they left the apartment and headed into town. Something was wearing off for her. Francis, sensing it, briefly squeezed the scruff of her neck, the way he knew she liked, and she leaned into his bulk. They walked down their street, the buildings around them radiating warmth from the day's sun, and emerged into the square.

It was busy, full of people sitting on the edge of the white stone fountain, or sitting at the tables of the restaurants surrounding it. Clara's gaze caught on the fountain's centrepiece: two lovers carved in an embrace above calm water. They picked the second restaurant they came to, sitting underneath a red parasol. A matching red glass ashtray, two red roses in a vase, a starched white tablecloth.

It's perfect, Clara said. It's just what I like. Just what I felt like. How did they know?

She sounded hysterical. His beautiful face swam before her.

Who? Francis asked.

She gestured at everything around them.

Francis stared at her, then opened his menu. Clara opened her own.

A fair-haired man came over with a basket of fresh, sweet-smelling bread, a small woman close behind him with a jug of water and a carafe of wine. Thank you, Francis told him, and Clara realized she had never seen him speak to another person until this strange holiday – a thing you would never normally even notice, a thing so taken for granted.

A life witnessed by two people only, made and remade, could be as real as anything witnessed and sanctified externally, she reminded herself. It exists. It exists only because we will it to exist, because we will it over and over, because there is no dailiness to take for granted when each day itself should not exist, snatched or conjured from time that belongs elsewhere.

All around her the sound and the light and the warmth existed. They existed. It was her belief made manifest.

What will you get? Francis asked her, lowering his menu.

The carbonara, she said. She felt faint.

Plates of beautiful food arrived quickly. The steam curled up from them. Somewhere a few tables away, a man rose up and smashed his wine glass to the floor. This did not seem strange to anyone else. A weeping blonde woman in a small red dress, holding a bunch of wilting yellow freesias, was escorted out by a waitress. Clara pushed away her plate.

Aren't you hungry? Francis asked, mouth full.

I'm feeling a bit unsettled, she said.

That's understandable, said Francis. He swallowed, put down his fork and reached out his hand to her.

It's just that I've been waiting so long for something – for *anything* – to happen, said Clara.

Francis looked around them, at the square. Well, he said. It seems like something has.

He looked suspicious suddenly. Was Clara imagining it, or had his tone cooled?

Are you blaming me? she asked.

Of course not, he said at once. How could you possibly have done this?

I don't know, she said, faltering. By wanting you too much? By not being satisfied with what I have?

But that's normal. He smiled. From the moment you leave my side I want you back. He paused, his eyes searching. That's part of what makes things so good, isn't it? Aren't you happy?

Clara looked back at him. I don't know, she said again, and as she said it, she realized it was true. Her feelings had become slippery, the line between pleasure and pain too blurred. She wanted Francis; every other feeling was experienced through the prism of that purpose.

Francis picked up his fork.

Well, I'm happy, he said. You make me very happy.

As Francis pulled this familiar statement out, the statement that could generally end all threat of discord between them, Clara remembered the times he had vanished for weeks, the times he had told her not to be in touch, the times when she had seemed disposable.

But the narrative of their complicity was hard to let go of. To unpick it would have felt too painful and too disloyal. Francis, standing behind a line that Clara had pulled him over, trying valiantly to pull himself back. Together they would dance along the length of the line for ever. It was not possible to cross into his world, and he would never permanently cross into hers. The inevitability of it felt exhausting all at once, though it was not new knowledge. She wanted to lay her head down on the table.

Instead, she watched the people crossing the square. One man moved alone through the couples, and she watched him walking faster than anyone else, as if propelled by fury or terror. He wanted to get home, she could sense, in case the person he loved had vanished, in case they were no longer existing peacefully in a room in a mysterious house or apartment where things were both not quite right and more right than they had ever been.

She saw the man spot a woman with red hair and speed up to reach her, falling into an embrace. Even from a distance, she could feel their relief.

Clara looked at Francis across the table for a long time.

Will I ever really have you? she asked eventually.

But you do have me, he said. In some of the best ways. Better than the usual.

Her eyes were beseeching.

Clara. Come on, he insisted, gently. With his fork he pricked her hand, so lightly she could barely feel it.

Is this real? Is any of this real? Or have I finally lost my mind? asked Clara, gesturing around at the bustling square.

Well, if you've lost your mind then I've lost mine too, he said. If this is a delusion, it's a shared one.

Like our entire relationship, she said.

Like love more generally, he said, not rising to the bait.

She let out a dark, low laugh that he had never heard before. Such a romantic, she said.

I thought you liked that.

I do.

So what's the matter with you?

Only that there's nothing in my life that's actually real, she said.

Stop being melodramatic, he said, his resolve slipping as he put his hands down on the table. All right. What I do know is that we are in love, and that is real. That is one of the only real things worth anything in the world.

Now who's being melodramatic, she said.

A waiter came to take their plates, leaving them with the menu again. Francis sat back in his chair. The narrative had also established from the start that his life was more difficult than hers, the stakes higher. He drained his wine in one long swill, and motioned for more.

Clara could feel the glasses of wine working inside her, queasy and thrilling. The city where she lived with Arturo, the real world, felt very far away. She had the loose sense that nothing material had changed, that it was still waiting for her, but she did not want to return to it. And it horrified her to think about how quickly she could renounce all else for Francis, how easily her life could be put to one side in favour of this unknown city. What she thought was real, what she took for granted as real, meant nothing after all, for next to him everything else fell away. And what did that mean for her life, she asked herself, the way she had done so many times before. What did that make it?

You're in a very good position yourself, you know, he said, watching her intently. You have almost total freedom.

I'm not free. I'm in a waiting room, she said.

I've never asked you to wait, he said at once.

Not explicitly, she said.

But you know that I love you, he said.

The wine arrived. They watched the waiter, blushing, pour it into their glasses in a long, bloody arc.

What comes afterwards? asked Clara, once he had left. Her voice was quieter.

Eternal devotion, or its ending at some point, said Francis.

He was so calm. It infuriated Clara.

You have all the answers, she said.

Actually, I don't have any. We're in uncharted territory.

Literally, said Clara. She started to laugh, but it turned, unexpectedly, into a sob. Francis put out his hand to her, but she shook it away.

Do you want to go home? she asked. Your real home, I mean. Do you really want to find a way out of this place?

A pause between them.

See, she said. You can't wait to be rid of me.

I don't want to leave, Francis replied. Even if I knew how to leave, I wouldn't want to.

But you'd want to go back sometime, she said.

He sighed.

Maybe, he said. Yes. Because I would miss them.

They fell silent. Around them, laughter. Clara balled up the cloth napkin in her hands. It was embroidered with tiny, alien red flowers. Francis was looking at her in a way she could not quite parse. He had receded from her, as if in a fog. Normally when he did this it would inspire panic, but now she felt reckless.

You've never been angry with me before, she said. We've never argued.

I've never wanted to waste our time together, he said. We have so little of it.

Well, here I am, she said. Wasting it.

Stop this, Clara, said Francis. Stop this.

His voice was level, but Clara noted, with a certain relish, the flush at the base of his neck.

A couple had sat down at the table next to them while they spoke. An older couple, both elegantly grey. Their feet were pressed together under the table. The woman's eyes were shining with what seemed like tears, or maybe it was just her eyes, or the light. She speared a forkful of crisp salad into her mouth.

Do you want dessert? Francis asked.

Just coffee. And limoncello. She raised her hand for the waiter, and her eyes were shining too.

Perhaps you should drink less, said Francis.

I'm on holiday.

As you wish.

I know you don't want things to change, she said.

She was trembling, exhilarated. Francis looked at her as if he wasn't quite sure who she was.

People change all the time. Things change all the time, he said.

And that's terrifying, said Clara. Nobody knows what they set in motion, or they wouldn't do it in the first place.

I would, said Francis. He grasped both her hands in a sudden, desperate motion.

I don't think I would, she said.

He let her hands go. She felt a small, sharp pain in her ankle – a mosquito – but she ignored it. The coffee arrived. The waiter lit their candle, sputtering white wax in a red glass holder that matched the ashtray. A long silence.

I'm sorry, she said eventually. I didn't mean it.

He smiled faintly, tired. I know, he said.

I love you, she said.

I know that too, he said.

She wanted to return to the museum where they had met and never follow him, to disregard him, to burn it down.

No, that wasn't right. The idea of her life without that day in it was untenable.

Something's stung me on my ankle, she said. Could you take a look?

Francis swung her foot up into his lap effortlessly, sandal and all. He examined the skin there, tracing it with his finger. A small red wound, perfectly circular, raw but not bleeding.

It must be a bite, he said. I don't know what from.

Clara looked around. Do you think there's anything poisonous here?

I have no idea, said Francis. Despite everything, he started to laugh.

Maybe I'll die, said Clara, starting to laugh too. Soon they were both bent double, tears streaming from their faces.

She looked at him across the table, the image of him blurred by the water beading her eyelashes. All around him people talked and ate and the waiters moved about, pouring more wine, and he was once more calm and implacable, and she never wanted to leave this place of amnesiac wonder, of unmoving sky.

The two red roses in the vase on the table had been vibrant when they sat down, but now they were faded and wrinkled. Clara took a petal between her fingers, studied it. It was as soft as skin.

I'm going to kiss you now, she said.

He leaned towards her so she could reach him over the table, so she could place her hands against his face, and it didn't matter if anybody saw. The sunset came down in a blaze of fiery pink, and the lights were coming on in the square, and for a while everybody was happy, and they did not think of judgement, or elsewhere, of being dead or alive. They did not think of very much at all.

How to summarize their life together in the other city, the time between the first museum and the last hotel?

Picture Clara sitting naked on the floor at Francis's feet, resting her head on his knee, an intimacy so unexpectedly pure that he wants to cry, but he doesn't show it. Pale cheek pressed to black twill. His hand, unringed, against the gentle scoop of her neck.

Picture Clara at the front desk of the gallery where she works, hamstrung by her desire, no word from Francis for weeks. *Perhaps he will walk in*, she thinks. *Perhaps he is dead*, she thinks. Either possibility seems equally violent, equally plausible.

Picture Francis hearing a popular love song on the radio, for the first time understanding it as language.

Picture Clara in the bath, touching each of her limbs with reverence in the same places he touched them with even more reverence. Here, here, and here. Kneecap transfigured. Her unremarkable shins. The elbow's rough patch.

Picture Francis spotting Clara in a crowd one Saturday morning in the supermarket when he is with his family and the sudden flood of adrenaline followed by calm, the emergency protocols, the gathering of the self, only to discover when she turns around it is not her at all. Ice cream, afterwards, for the three of them. Abundance, gratefulness, his hands shaking on the cone.

Picture an afternoon bed. Gold light, dim.

I would pause time right here, Francis tells Clara as they lie on the bed, looking into each other's eyes. This moment above all other moments.

Rain and thunder outside. His long, warm body pressed to hers. *Let me always return to this place gladly, whatever else happens in the world*, Clara asks silently. *Please.*

Return

Clara woke up alone. She lay still for a moment. The blind of her window wasn't fully unrolled, letting in a sliver of tepid light at the bottom. She shut her eyes, counted to three, but when she opened them she was still there. Her sheets were rumpled and cold. Clothes on the floor that she had not put away. There was no other body there. She got up, searched the familiar kitchen, the familiar bathroom. The apartment was empty.

At the other end of this city, Francis woke next to his wife. He was alerted to the change by the total darkness, the blackout curtains she favoured. For a moment, unable to see, he panicked. He turned to the warmth of the body sleeping in the bed next to him, and put out a hand. Clara, he said out loud. The body was slighter; his hand landed on the strap of a nightgown he had chosen. He froze. His wife continued to sleep. Within her sleep she had heard the mistake, the invocation – *Clara* – and decided to absorb it as a dream. Next door, their daughter started to sing.

Clara stood in the steaming, too-hot jet of the shower. She checked her phone, expecting missed calls from work, but there was nothing. It was a Sunday, somehow. Arturo must have been elsewhere, waking up in someone else's bed, and she was powerfully glad to be alone. She washed each limb with methodical precision. The strange wound at her ankle stung under the soap and water. It was the only thing that confirmed she had not imagined it all.

Francis made eggs in the kitchen for the three of them. He felt drugged, dislocated. Normally after leaving Clara, he had some time to absorb the loss, to switch from one version of himself back to the other. He was glad of the distraction of cooking, of how it felt to crack shells viciously into the pan and stir their yolks and watch them alchemize.

Clara lay back on her bed and focused on the patch of paint above her that was peeling. She thought of Francis and his wife and his daughter together in a house whose shapes and surfaces she did not know, but which she had spent much time imagining. Eventually she went out to the coffee shop near her house, where they recognized her and spoke to her easily and gave no sign that they had noticed any absence. She walked to the park and sat there with tears streaming down her face. Although the sun was shining, how insipid it seemed after the other city; how paltry the very air, how dirty the roads, with the cars screaming and burning their way into the distance.

After breakfast, Francis examined the calendar that hung in the kitchen, marked with appointments and birthdays. *Swimming!* underlined, written in felt tip, the day before. He had gone to sleep on the Saturday night, lived entire days in the other city – yet here he was, as if nothing had taken place.

He turned his attention to his daughter, who was demanding he play with her. He was trembling, he realized, still somehow waiting for acknowledgement of his recent absence, his outrageous abandonment, but none came. Time had either been frozen or dialled back, stripped of its consequence.

His wife found the two of them putting together a puzzle in another room. There were so many rooms in his beautiful house. There was no recrimination.

Clara's feet took her to the museum where she had met Francis. It was crowded. In front of *Still Life with Cherries and Mouse* she sat on a small velvet sofa. An old man sat next to her. Clara hated the old man for not being Francis, though he was kindly, with tufted soft white hair like a baby's. She hated the painting too – the self-satisfied, artful little arrangement, the smug array of plenty. She tried to call up the version of herself who had followed Francis when he was still a stranger. But she had been rewired, she felt. Love had remade her, had refigured those versions of herself, and she felt a new grief at this. That was the risk you took in the process of transformation: you would never be that person again. She felt blunted with the loss, a knife chipped on a stone.

Francis had scared her a little when she first met him, with his poise that could read as coldness, even arrogance. But it turned out that this intimidating man was actually quite gentle, and then she came to love that she knew this about him. She still didn't know his daughter's name, but she knew he liked having his head scratched when he laid it in her lap, that he was deathly afraid of wasps, that he had never eaten an oyster or broken a bone, that he had hit six foot by thirteen and lost his virginity in the unhappy year after. He was much stranger than he seemed, increasingly beautiful when closely studied, and he didn't seem to mind that Clara was quite stupid, that she was impulsive and shallow, that she rarely did anything of note. He didn't seem to mind her ordinariness. Perhaps it was the strength of her desire that overcame it – that elevated the experience of loving her to something else, some gleaming and golden promise.

I like being your object, Francis had told her at the start of their relationship, emailing her at work. She had been at her last job, the one before the gallery, one where she performed brisk admin in a brightly lit office, exposed. Her work was embarrassing, unnecessary. His seemed good and pure. She thought of him describing painters of four hundred years past to a rapturous audience. Her fingers moved on the keyboard, switching between spreadsheet and him. She did not deserve him, she felt. It was incredible that he wanted her, she felt.

Reduce me to parts, he wrote.

Gladly, she replied.

Long legs, shoulder's curve, smooth cock, cheekbone, hands. She memorized him, as if he were an exam subject. She did her best with the temporary version that was on offer to her.

Late-afternoon rain across the city. Francis and his family sat together, watching a film. He thought about Clara incessantly, but could not bring himself to go out, to drive to her house and look through her window, illuminated slightly, the shadow of her just visible. He fell back on easy excuses with some shame. The weather; the family unit.

He rang his mother. Francisco, she said. Ten years ago she had moved back to the small Spanish village where he had been raised, though the move still felt new to him. He liked to think of her there, liked this long-gone version of himself reflected in the name he rarely used. Francisco was the solemn child who built things with tin cans and string and who had thrown stones at birds, who had watched the girls in the house across the road when the curtains were not drawn fully.

Clara waited for him to find her. She could never contact him first. That was the inviolate rule. Instead she drank with determination in the half-light of the apartment, red wine, sitting on the edge of the chair in the corner of the living room. Grey water sluiced the windows. She was alone. Her phone chirruped weakly from the coffee table: a text from Arturo. *Weekend got away with me. Will fill you in tomorrow. Or Tuesday?? Love you xxx*. Her hands gripped the glass. She did not understand. She had been given what she had always wanted, and it had been taken away. A brief, delirious dream. Better not to have seen it, she thought. Better not to have known.

Francis went to bed shortly after his daughter did, citing a headache. He said he would sleep in a spare room, so as not to be disturbed. His wife agreed, and kissed him on the cheek. He lay awake for a long time.

Across the city, Clara removed her clothes. She had been wearing white socks, and she noticed that the insect bite had opened and bled through on to them. She contemplated putting them in her laundry basket, but instead wrapped the socks in a plastic bag and put them in a drawer, as if gathering evidence.

When they opened their eyes the next morning they were back in the apartment in the other city, waking to the patterns of light on the ceiling, to the presence of the body of the other. They gripped each other in fervour. Francis felt afraid, and glad. Clara promised, silently, to be good.

Did they notice you were gone? she said.

No, he said. Everything was as it always was.

Francis pushed his face into Clara's neck and breathed a long, shuddering breath.

Did you miss me?

I missed you so very much.

Home

They had only been gone a day, after all. The peaches they had bought were still waiting on the counter. Their favourite clothes hung in the wardrobe, more of them, freshly laundered. The sky was the same uninterrupted blue.

He put his head between her thighs. He moved slowly, more slowly still, stopping for a moment now and then to look at her closely, his face devout, his mouth gentle as he hooked his fingers inside her body. Please, she said, the only word left to her, the only language she still could form – *please* – and she arched her back involuntarily, and a sharp noise that she only dimly recognized as belonging to her rang out, and it was unbearable, she thought, to know such pleasure, for she didn't know how she could live with it, live with knowing it existed, knowing it could be taken away at any moment.

Afterwards she was flushed, elsewhere. He lay there, with his arms clasped around her hips, until the early-morning light changed. He listened to her breathing as if he were listening out for an animal, his cheek pressed to her smooth abdomen.

They left the building more confidently this time, and the winding streets they staked out felt more familiar. They passed the fountain of the lovers in their embrace, the stall selling the cones of fried courgette flowers. They didn't talk about the real world, about the stilled time. They didn't ask *why*, or *how*.

They discovered a new square, this one pitched with a market, bustling and good-smelling. Here they bought lemons and parsley, fresh cream and warm bread and huge bulbs of lavender-tinted garlic. In the green-fronted grocer's shop they had visited before, they bought anchovies and spaghetti and good olive oil. When they arrived home, they placed the lemons in a white ceramic bowl that Clara had not noticed before. It was the first time they had ever cooked a meal together. Francis put his hands around Clara's waist as they waited for the pasta to boil. She leaned back into him and closed her eyes.

Every beautiful thing was a testimony. Every beautiful thing said, *You have been right to live like this.* She had been *right* to believe in what exists when not seen, she had been *right* to believe in flimsiness, she had been *right* to believe in what left no proof except in her own body, a fingertip bruise on the wrist, a charcoal pencil, the ambiguous morsels she had accumulated. Her waiting was bearing fruit. She had believed, and now she was receiving the abundance.

She opened her eyes and it was all still there. The light, diced in buttery cubes on the floor. Francis moving to the stove, hooking a hot strand of pasta out with his finger and wincing. The counter was solid, the juice of the lemon she cut sharp. Inside herself, Clara was changing. It was evident to her, and to her alone. She was being given more than she had thought possible. Her body soaked it up. She felt submerged in bliss.

Sometimes, in the hotels, they had liked to play at being in the world. The sheets were a lake they swam through. The carpet grass and foliage, lush between splayed fingers as they crouched, drunk, on their knees, on their stomachs, laughing. The lamps were rare plants and trees. The sheets of monogrammed paper and sachets of milk, sugar, salt were artefacts, and the robes were evening gowns, and the glasses they drank wine and water from were the glasses of a restaurant, the polished wood table at the foot of the bed the place where their plates were set.

And the shower was a rainstorm that nourished the ground on which they walked, so that things could grow. And the curtains were swaying leaves, or shopfronts, or waves. And the windows were keeping them safe from all that threatened to encroach: the wild animals, ferocious weather, natural disaster. But there, in the room, they were safe. They could pull the covers over their heads and wait for the worst to happen, for the world to wash over them in all its inconsequential glory.

Francis lay awake that night and once again broached the question of *why*, and the question of *how*.

What brings us here? he asked, not aloud, not to Clara, but to the city itself. *And what drives us away?*

But the city did not answer.

Beside him, Clara silently asked the city to keep him with her, to never let them leave. She asked the vines on the rug in the living room to come to life and clutch at his feet. She asked for the gaps in the floorboards to widen into ravines, so that he might fall in. She asked for the bedding to twist like ropes at his ankles, his wrists. *I will do anything if I can only stay*, she vowed. *Anything.*

Each morning they woke up to a different pattern in the sky, frozen, as if painted. One of them would make the coffee and bring it back to bed. They took it in turns to lead the day's explorations, lead the other through the city, making of it a game. On the days when she followed Francis, obediently, wherever he wanted to take her, Clara was reminded of their first meeting. He was bolder than her, walked faster and further. She was slower, more observant, bought a notebook and pencil in order to sketch a kind of map of the city: a project soon abandoned, once she realized how impossible it was.

For the city was fluid, cohesive and yet disparate, so that one moment they were walking up a street of narrow stairs bordered by worn high buildings, and the next they had turned on to a wide, paved boulevard lined with benches on which couples sat, listening to two busking accordionists surrounded by scattered gold coins. It was difficult to know whether the buildings and sights were actually new, freshly invented details springing up all the time around them, or whether they simply hadn't noticed them before. Either way, Clara was determined to become familiar with it all, to witness and remember it, now that it was hers. The windows lit by candles at night, the fountains glittering with the coins of so many wishes (so much of the same wish), the clattering of the metro below their feet, the couples kissing in their finery. She imprinted the images on her mind with a studied dedication.

The city was not as small as it had seemed on that first day. They only reached the outskirts again once, turning around an unassuming corner to be confronted with the expanse of redness and water right ahead of them. There were other couples on the shore that time. The tide seemed to be out, the sand gleaming, and the others were far away from Clara and Francis, right up to the line of the sea, if it *was* a sea. Clara felt an instinctive, inexplicable revulsion at the idea of wet red sand graining her shoes, even as she wondered what the water might have left behind – strange jellyfish dredged from the depths, seaweed and shell. Though maybe there was only the prosaic detritus that you could find on any ordinary beach. Maybe it was better not to find out.

Whether the city was a mere imitation of life, or life's analogue, was still unclear. But what did it matter when the restaurants were fine and well lit, the weather bright, the streets free of litter, and the deals brokered by the inhabitants impossible, shot through with unbelievable joy?

They made love most often in the afternoons, afternoons of infinite and supple hours, the way they usually had in the real city. Clara always felt embarrassed describing it as *making love*, though it seemed the most accurate term. She could just call it *fucking*, she decided eventually, because even the ugliest word possible wouldn't detract from the beauty of the act, wouldn't cheapen its intensity of purpose, intensity of feeling. Clara could feel their souls, or something like them, moving between them. She also felt embarrassed referring to a *soul*, even internally, but she didn't know what other term to use, for their fucking placed her entirely in herself and beyond herself, and she felt an incommunicable gratitude that she had been able to discover it, for whatever coincidences and machinations had – miraculously – brought body to bear on body.

One day they found a new metro station, this one called *Central*, just past the square with the fountain. They went down the steps with some confusion. Inside, it smelled of new paint, the tiled floors pristine. They pushed through the idle turnstiles, and within minutes a small train arrived, the seats carpeted in orange and brown. They looked at each other as if they had never seen a train before. Should we get on? Clara asked, already taking a step forward. The doors closed as soon as they were aboard.

Clara kept looking out of the windows, though all there was to see was total darkness. The fluorescent lights flickered as they hit a rattling stretch of track. Francis held her hand, stroked her knuckles with the rough ball of his thumb.

They passed Park, then City North, then River Central. Francis made no move to get up. Clara grew impatient. Let's get off here, she said, as they pulled into a stop marked *City East*.

There was a small museum right next to the station. From outside, it looked almost identical to the one in which they had met. Inside, the sandstone floor was the same, the vaulting roof was the same. But the exhibits were different, classified according to no order they could understand, and with no signs to explain.

What is this? Francis asked in the second room, examining a twisted sculpture of cobalt-coloured glass, air bubbles trapped here and there.

I don't know, said Clara. You're the historian.

She moved to a tapestry nearby, feeling drawn to it. She studied the birds and the deer sewn into fabric, the threads unravelling near the bottom. A pulse of recognition, then nothing. She wished she could say something clever or important about it to Francis, but her mind was blank.

The other visitors looked at the objects with similar puzzlement. There was meaning somewhere, but it moved from her grasp like a dream half-remembered. Clara saw a woman in a long red skirt grip on to the arm of her companion, a short man in a white shirt, as they came to a small piano cast in gold. Was it beautiful? She was too far away to see. Francis walked ahead of Clara, pausing in the doorway of the next room in order to watch her. Loose white T-shirt, arms strong, long dark hair tied back today with a pale ribbon – where had she found such a thing? he wondered, marvelling at this detail, at how easily she seemed able to adapt to anything. Already she was a creature of this city, comfortable in a way that he was not. Her step was quick, her gaze inquisitive. She sensed him looking and turned to meet his eyes, flashed him a brilliant smile. He longed to touch her as she walked towards him then past him, and then realized – incredibly – that he could. He could touch her whenever he liked, in front of anyone. He reached out to the ribbon, stroked it lightly. She stopped at once. His hand moved to her shoulder. Underneath the T-shirt, she was running warm.

They passed a cabinet of books preserved under glass. Displays of furniture, of ceramics, of fabrics pressed neatly and framed in compact, uniform squares. They paused only at the entrance to the last room, the smallest room. It was windowless, empty except for a single painting displayed prominently on the opposite wall, lights set above it. *Still Life with Cherries and Mouse.* Larger than they remembered, the colours more vivid.

A reproduction, Francis said, to himself more than anyone. It must be.

Clara didn't care that it wasn't the original, felt only an overwhelming joy to see it. She had to fight the impulse to run up to the canvas and press her lips to it.

Would you have followed me if we had met in front of another painting? she asked.

Yes, Francis said. I would have followed you if I had seen you anywhere.

Nobody else came in for a long time as they stood there, taking the familiar objects in like they were new. Bread and artichoke and fruit, the pewter jug, the knife laid down. The colours seemed to throb, the food almost overripe. The mouse looked alert, as if it could run from the frame.

She could never tell whether she loved the painting because it was how she had met Francis, or if she loved it on its own merits. It was difficult to disentangle the two. Love for the object itself, or for what the object represented.

But she loved how the anonymous painter was visible if you looked very, very closely at the pewter jug: a tiny, stretched reflection.

She loved that mouse, so sly and well fed and beady-eyed, intent on taking what it could.

She loved the idea of the painter eating almonds the way that she, too, ate almonds, almost four hundred years in the future – palmed right into her mouth, carelessly.

She loved the window into a world recognizable and unrecognizable, the objects venerated, mystical, becoming more than just themselves.

Clara could not shake the feeling that there was something different about the painting here, something that had previously gone unnoticed. She stepped closer, frowned. There was a single bite missing from one of the apples at the back, each tooth-mark lovingly defined. Before she could point this out to Francis, the woman in the red skirt wandered in with her partner, breaking the spell. They looked at the painting with little interest; it meant nothing to them.

They ordered coffee in the museum cafeteria, identical to the cafe in the real museum. The sun fell in a stripe across the hollow of Clara's neck as she sipped it. Francis couldn't take his eyes off her. He felt an unwelcome shadow at the edge of his good mood, wanted only to lie in her adoring arms for the rest of the afternoon in order to stave it off.

Let's go home, he said.

Home, home, home. Clara closed her eyes.

Say it again, she said, without opening them.

Home, he said.

On their way back, they passed a florist's and she bought a spray of yellow roses wrapped in brown paper, roses so preternaturally beautiful that it was hard to believe they had been grown, presumably, from the earth. They started to wilt as soon as they left the shop. Back in the apartment, she spooned sugar into a large vase, a pinch of salt. Improvised plant food. Francis loved her for this, for the care she demonstrated as she trimmed the ends of the stems, the bright and nervous motions of her hands. She was loose water through his fingers, shimmering.

If anything, Clara's efforts seemed to kill the roses faster. They browned and then died almost immediately, petals dropping, even as Francis watched her watching them. She looked towards him, her face blank, and he took it between his hands. Never mind, he said. He kissed her deeply. He pressed her against the counter, lifted her body up.

But Clara was a student of bargaining, and so she wondered if the universe might notice her efforts regardless; if it might grant her some grace in return, whatever form it took.

That evening she insisted on running Francis a bath, on washing his hair with her own hands. Flickering candlelight, white wax and glass blue from night's fall, the steam curling up against it. They were sweet with each other, drunk on each other's presence. She felt her fingers move through the soap suds with a sort of disbelief. There it was, his skull, held between her palms like an egg. His body held by her body. She kissed his wet ear. She wound a curl around her finger.

And Francis really did feel, somewhere, that all was right with the world.

In the real city, after spending time with Francis, everything had made a new kind of sense to Clara. He was a shortcut into beauty that she had never imagined.

She paid attention to the tiniest, most ordinary things. She marvelled at the grace with which they had been brought into existence, at how it all fitted together. An orange's long, sinuous peel. A small dog, running along the pavement. Ray of sunshine. The splash of colour left from a poster carelessly pasted to a wall, the rest of the paper worn down to the brick. She saw it all. Devotion to the world. To see it, to record it — this refiguring, this making-new, together and apart. She let the ordinary reveal its secret lustre, hazed with goodness as if with heat.

She felt sure she would never grow tired of looking at his body, stretched out before her on a bed, or as he sat in a chair. An interlude, half-dressed, eyes out of the window. The curve of shoulder, of bicep. The rise and fall of his ribs. How carefully he had been made, as if designed for her alone. How thoughtful the details.

Their second meeting, Clara naked on the ground at his feet while he was mostly dressed, her cheek against his knee. Tell me about the objects in the painting, she said, looking up at him. Francis knew more about it than she did, though he too could not disentangle it from the first moment he had seen her, despite the fact that his knowledge of the painting preceded his knowledge of her. It had been recontextualized.

She felt milk-fed, replete with her luck.

You want me to sing for my supper? he asked.

She smiled lazily, in affirmation. He thought about it for a moment.

All right. So we have fruits of paradise, most obviously and importantly, he said. Earthly temptation, pleasures, and time's inevitable passing. Also Body of Christ, possibly. Probably.

So dramatic, said Clara.

It seemed best to avoid interpreting *fidelity* for the burning candle, he thought, as she shifted against his leg.

What about the mouse? she asked.

Oh, he's just there to remind us that nothing lasts, he said.

But he's so sweet, she said.

He's a threat, Francis said. He wants his dinner.

Clara laughed, a low chuckle deep in her throat that he felt in his own body.

And of course the artichoke's *heart* is revealed, he said, emboldened. Cut in half, served up on the plate.

She was quiet.

Though I prefer to think that there are meanings we could never possibly decipher fully, he continued, a little too quickly, stroking her hair. A message in a bottle, long disintegrated, for people we'll never know. It feels more pleasing than just thinking of it as something we can reduce to easy symbolism. Or as a pretty display.

But sometimes beauty can be enough, Clara said.

She felt embarrassed by her earnestness, but the simplicity of this statement pleased him more than anything else she could have said. He moved his hand to the soft spot of her neck, below her ear. She closed her eyes. Quiet. Warmth. His thumb, gentle, against her pulse. It beat quickly.

Maybe it was a message meant for future lovers, she said. Or we can just give the objects our own meaning, if we want. She opened her eyes and rose to her knees, started to unbutton his shirt.

We already have, he said, hands moving to her waist. And now they are ours.

The owners of the green shop – Paula and Jean – had started to greet her on sight. She leaned her elbows on the counter and watched Jean as he shuffled the bottles behind the counter, brushing the dust from them. Paula was checking the till, making little piles of gold coins.

How long have you been here? Clara asked.

A long time, said Paula. I forget. It's not that important.

She had a wonderful shock of silver hair that fell to her shoulders. Jean was younger, with close-cropped ashy hair and deep wrinkles at his eyes.

And you, you're new, she said. We've noticed you.

She stepped back towards Jean, elbowed him in the side. Jean looked up and raised his eyebrows.

And your other? he asked. Clara hesitated, then pointed through the doorway to where Francis was just visible, standing in a patch of light. Turned away, shifting on his feet as if to invisible music, unaware of her gaze. Waiting for her, she thought, incredulous. She put two ice creams in pink wrappers on the counter, one gold coin.

Does everyone have an *other* here? she asked.

They do, he replied, taking the coin. Clara waited for an explanation, but none came.

Both Paula and Jean looked somewhat unearthly, as if they had come through a long illness. Their limbs bore shiny pink wounds, healed over. Jean put his arms around Paula, an embrace that made Clara feel both uncomfortable and glad to witness.

She was unlikely to grow old with Francis. She had known that from the start. But Paula and Jean appeared to be doing so. And when she walked back outside into a wall of hot light, there he was, still waiting, smiling at her. She felt such incredible joy as the force of the sun hit her. The sky was so blue, with its unmoving, sentimental clouds! The pavement was so clean! If she didn't want to ask any questions, she simply didn't have to ask them. She could just ignore them and turn her head up to the sky. She could sit on that bench over there, she thought, and Francis would sit next to her, and they would eat their ice cream as other people moved past them together in their pairs, walking or jogging. She could sit, and she could let the radiance of her life move through her in all its bewildering and soporific truth. She dimly felt the hard edges of logic somewhere, but the heat was so compelling, and the presence of Francis next to her, his arm in his thin cotton shirt pressed to hers, soothed her the way it always did. It felt more real than many things she knew for sure to be real.

A new shop had appeared just outside the main square, a cycle hire shop, all the bicycles an identical sunflower yellow. They could see so much more of the city this way, Clara thought with excitement, pushing her bike on to the cobbles. Francis wanted to cycle along the river, to see where it might lead, whereas Clara wanted to go back to the hill they found on their first visit. But in the end she didn't mind where they went. Francis turned left and right and left again. The city felt slippery around her, blurred. She stood up on the pedals, let the wind move through her hair.

They reached the river and carried on beside it, moving downstream. Clara expected they would find its end quickly, but it was longer, much longer, than she would have thought from their previous explorations. She imagined the city stretching itself out constantly, further and further, like an exploding star. New iterations, new embellishments. They passed underneath bridges of elegant brick, which gave way to bridges of metal and glass and concrete, all bearing couples hand in hand. Sometimes the river widened so much that Clara thought they must surely be coming to its mouth, but then it would narrow again and continue, shaded by overhanging trees, the cool air coming up off its surface.

They stopped by a stone water fountain set off the path, propping their bicycles against a spindly, naked tree. Francis cupped his hands and drank, then put his head under the flow of water. He stood up and shook his head like a dog.

Could it be possible that the city had no bicycles until now? he wondered aloud.

Anything's possible, said Clara. Maybe it wants us to explore. Maybe it's pushing us.

She was starting to think of the city as an animal, something whose stomach they were living in, a breathing and reactive organism. It watched them and it tested them, though whether benevolently or not, she wasn't sure. Either way, the idea was comforting to Clara.

As they cycled on, the buildings on either side of the river spread out, the foliage overhanging the path growing sparse. The air started to feel thinner in their lungs. They no longer passed people on the path, or saw them on the opposite bank. Then the river widened very suddenly into a silted terracotta beach. They were back at the sea that surrounded them.

They pushed the bicycles on to the sand, taking in the

curved bay, the water dark and viscous with an occasional wave breaking on the gravel. The tide wasn't out so far as the last time. Other couples walked along the shoreline; not many, but a few.

They sat down on the red earth and stretched out their legs. Together they looked at the horizon. The sky was a fainter blue at its edges, hazed over.

If it was clearer, do you think we could see further? Francis asked.

There might not be that much to see, Clara replied.

There's always something, said Francis.

She watched him gaze intently at the horizon.

I fancy a swim, he said.

Are you insane? Clara replied, astonished.

Come on, he said, already pulling off his T-shirt, revealing damp patches under the arms which Clara found appealing — love was so pathological! she chastised herself lightly — and then he was just in his boxers, standing up, and walking swiftly towards the water without waiting for her. Don't go too far! she called.

He waded in up to his waist, standing there for a while, seemingly to gather courage. Then, as if deciding something, he plunged right in, and then he became very small very quickly. Clara felt the familiar tug in her chest, keeping him carefully within her eyeline. The water looked deep but calm, more like a lake than anything. She had never seen him swim before, didn't know if he was good at it, but it turned out he was, moving smoothly through the dark water. A whole new set of gestures; she filed the information away with a little shiver of happiness.

She turned her attention to the other couples on the beach. Two older women, walking up and down the same small patch of shoreline rapidly, staring at the ground as if they were looking for something lost. A young man and woman, leaning low to the ground as they skipped stones. Smooth, flat pebbles in their hands, ready to be sent across the surface. They travelled a long way, longer than Clara would have thought possible, past where Francis was swimming. Perhaps the stones could reach the real world, create an echo that would breach its confines. Someone somewhere, on another body of water, would see the ripples without understanding what they meant. Or maybe they would understand. Maybe, sometimes, a message was sent, and found purchase.

Was it cold? she asked when he returned, dripping.
    A little, he said. At first.
    Weren't you afraid of sea monsters?
    No, he said.
    Why not?
    I know those things aren't real.
    He sat next to Clara, panting.
    Maybe you want to rethink your logic, she said. She kissed his wet cheek. He smelled of brine, of any unremarkable water.

They didn't cycle back along the river, but went directly into the city on the roads, joining a growing stream of yellow bicycles heading into the centre. As they approached the heart of the city, the cyclists in front of them slowed. They could hear music, and whistles, and shouting. People started jumping off their bikes, abandoning them at the side of the road, looking around to find the source of the commotion. Francis dismounted, wheeling his bike, and Clara copied him. They moved towards the sounds.

As they turned a corner they saw the crowd of people, faces painted with glitter, colourful paper streamers draped around their shoulders, surging down the street. At the front of the group was a ragtag musical band carrying flutes, violins, recorders; two women had drums looped around their necks. Clara and Francis hung back for only a moment before joining the party, Clara clapping and laughing with delight like a child.

The crowd flowed and pulled them through the streets that she was beginning to know, beginning to love. The squares of parks, laid out with rose bushes and arboretums, neat lawns and winding paths. Flashes of water. Pools and fountains and ornamental sculpture, cobblestones polished with age by countless feet. More people joined their number, and those who didn't join watched beaming from the sides, or waved down from their balconies, or from the restaurant tables where they ate their lunches, drank their coffees and their wines.

Someone blew their whistle too close to Clara's ear, then apologized – *sorry!* he shouted, a young man with blonde, gelled spikes of hair, holding hands with a woman with blue and black hair and a septum piercing – but Clara didn't mind. I'm Jay, and this is Ima, the blonde man said, handing over the whistle in a kind of apology, it's good to meet you, and Clara smiled at him and accepted the whistle, and Ima gave her a big, dreamy hug, left her arm slung around her shoulder. I'm Clara, she said, and this is Francis, and it felt so good, so ordinary, to introduce him, and Jay hugged Francis the way Ima had hugged her. And Clara blew the whistle hard and long, so that Jay and Ima and Francis all whooped. She took a deep breath, paused, then blew it harder still.

They were forever finding new gardens, new places in which to lie down on the grass in the long and lazy afternoons, talking and kissing until their lips were swollen and they had to run home with desire – sometimes not even making it home but on their way finding a patch of sudden, implausibly long grass, or a roomy cafe bathroom, or a forgiving, slyly designed recess or alley in which to slake their ardour. One afternoon their explorations led them to the best park yet – vast and green and full of immaculate, intricate topiary, fragrant tunnels of trailing wisteria, walled herb gardens. Clara exclaimed involuntarily at everything they saw: the flower beds voluptuous with poppies, the salmon pink of a tiny stone folly sandwiched in a sunny corner, a tree laden with cherries that couples were picking from, working together to reach the unspoiled fruit. At some point that day, Francis had stopped acknowledging her delight, but she couldn't prevent it from overspilling regardless.

He had woken up with a needling sensation at the temples and the image of his daughter clearly imprinted on his mind like an accusation; had allowed himself a moment in the bathroom to press his forehead against the tiles and cry a few hot, helpless tears. To return to Clara in the bedroom after that – guileless, happy, free, entirely unappreciative of that freedom – filled him with both comfort and contempt. Another day ahead of them of petting, giggling, lying around. It seemed insubstantial suddenly, though only the day before he had felt he could do it for ever.

They came to a lake full of rowing boats, gliding serenely across the water. Queuing up at the hire hut, the couple ahead of them in the line turned around and smiled. They looked familiar, and Francis placed them as the women from their first day in the city, the redhead and the mousy one with their toppling tower of sugar.

Have you been on one of these before? Clara asked them.

Not these ones specifically, replied the red-haired woman. We found them last time, but we didn't get a chance to have a go.

Last time you were in the park? asked Francis.

Last time we were in the city, she said.

So you also move back and forth? asked Clara, fascinated.

Oh yes, said her companion. Doesn't everyone?

I didn't know, Clara admitted. We're new.

So are we, said the red-haired woman. But you know, some people have been coming here for years.

Years! exclaimed Clara. Francis glanced uneasily at her.

How many times have you returned? he asked.

This is our third visit, said the mousy woman. And you?

Our second, said Clara.

How have you found it?

Wonderful, breathed Clara. Francis glanced at her again.

Yes, great, said Francis. Strange, but good.

They were at the front of the queue; the women stepped gently into their boat and were pushed off, into the water, waving. Clara and Francis's boat came next. They watched the couple in it – older, well-to-do – clamber out with some difficulty, wet patches on their clothes, eyes joyful.

In the boat Clara was distracted by watching the others on the water. Francis felt overstimulated, bewildered by the constant activity around them. Images of his daughter continued to enter his mind, unbidden. How she looked in sleep, flushed, her hands curled into fists the way she had done since she was a baby. The funny prim way she would request an apple cut into slices; the ragged, high-pitched line of her laugh when he put on a stupid voice, when he lifted her into the air. He pushed each image away carefully. He missed her so much, he realized, feeling sick. He had never been away from her for so long. But was he truly *away*? his conscience attempted to reason. If she would not notice his absence? And besides didn't he, too, have a right to his own life, his own happiness and adventures?

He did his best to concentrate on propelling them around the lake, but Clara's rowing was half-hearted, and she soon lost her oar.

Oh, she said, watching as it floated, not moving to catch it. Francis lunged and managed to save it, his shirt splashed with dirty water in the process, and when Clara laughed he felt a surge of disproportionate annoyance.

You're like a child, he said.

What do you mean? she asked, taking the oar from him and dipping it back into the water, inexpertly.

Someone's always there to look after you. You never have to do anything you don't want to do, he said.

I do a lot of things I don't want to do, she said.

No, you don't. Somehow you always get your way, he said.

She looked at him, hurt.

I thought you liked doing things for me, she said.

Not when you're selfish, or lazy, he said, moving the oar smoothly through the water.

Am I often those things? Clara asked.

Quite often, yes, he said.

They rowed in silence for a while. Clara started to cry, unexpectedly, without breaking the rhythm of their rowing. She could not bear the idea that he was displeased with her, as if she had failed some kind of test. Her face was scrunched up, and Francis's annoyance transformed without warning into livid anger. He was stuck with her, he thought – this capricious, bruisable person. He felt cheated, slung the oar into the bottom of the boat.

I want to go back to the shore, she said.

Stop crying, he said. It's pathetic.

Clara thrashed her oar into the water. The boat spun in circles. Two elegant men in striped shirts stared as they moved past in their own boat, languorous, aligned. They had a bottle of champagne in an ice bucket, a basket of strawberries.

I'll jump in! she threatened. I'll swim!

Fine, said Francis, leaning back. Keep making a scene. I don't care.

She gave up on the oar, clattering it into the bottom of the boat next to his, and wrapped her arms around herself. Above them, the sky changed colour as if a projector slide had been clicked discreetly into place; it was tinted with grey now, a change so small that Clara wondered if she had imagined it.

They didn't speak for a while, as the boat floated aimlessly. Eventually Francis raised his own oar and put it back in the water.

Come on, he said.

They rowed in silence. She was crying again by the time

they arrived at the shore. The others waiting in the queue looked on with alarm as she threw both oars on to the ground and walked off into the park rapidly, trying to put distance between them, but she soon had to slow, nausea taking hold of her. She felt trapped. Francis was behind her – resenting her, she felt, hating her. She felt her own rage rising up. She spun around to face him.

You're so cold, she said. Why are you doing this?

You were behaving like a child, he said.

Well, you'd know all about that, wouldn't you, she said.

Francis stopped at once.

Don't you dare talk about her, he said. Don't you dare talk about them.

You're just about ready to go back to them, I imagine, Clara said, and it was her turn to be cold this time, an icy transformation that took his breath away with a mixture of surprise, admiration, even desire. He kicked at a clod of earth, half-expecting it to reveal a concrete floor underneath. Clara was right. He felt, very strongly all of a sudden, an urge to return to life – to *real life*, he thought, not this manic procession of images, the couples laughing and screaming and kissing around them. He imagined reaching up to the sky and punching through, tearing it, flimsy as paper between his hands.

I don't expect you to understand what it's like, he said. Having a family. Having responsibilities.

Clara put her hand on her chest involuntarily. She smiled.

Because I'm not a middle-aged suburban father? she asked.

He refused to let her see how that winded him.

You've been on your best behaviour the whole time we've been here, he said.

So have you, she replied.

Clearly it's not sustainable, he said.

No, she said, and she was sobbing yet again now, really sobbing, and she looked at him with panic.

He felt a sudden pain on the back of his hand. Flinching, distracted, he glanced at it for only a moment. A wound, like the one Clara had received before, the sting of some unknown insect.

When they arrived at the apartment he locked himself in the bathroom and stayed in there for a long time. He did not answer Clara's tentative taps at the door, and when they stopped he felt guilty, but vindictive at the same time. He had lost patience — already he felt a little ashamed of himself — yes, lost patience with her, but perhaps also with the city itself, how it presented him with the binary facts of his own life so starkly. Family, duty, love, in one world; passion, friendship and a different, but real, love in another. Couldn't one have everything in the same place? What would it be like, to also have duty, maybe even a family, with Clara? He closed his eyes, struck by a quick pain again at his temples. He opened them, shook himself. It wasn't as if people never got divorced. But his daughter was so young. And he *liked* his family life, mostly, in ways that he could never have predicted. The little routines, the stable foundation. His wife was a good person, easy to live with; there had never been any great ruptures or tests, at least until now. For all he knew, she was having her own dalliances. Could she, too, be shuttling back and forth between cities real and unreal? Even the baseless possibility of it gave him some relief. His thoughts felt strewn around, disordered.

From the sofa Clara heard him leave the bathroom, the soft sound of his clothes hitting the floor as he undressed, then she saw the light extinguished.

Somehow he fell asleep. Clara didn't understand how. She approached the bed after some time had passed, once she was sure he wouldn't wake up, and stared at him in the dull blue light that bled around the curtains. The set of his mouth was hard even in sleep. A stranger.

She stood upon the balcony and watched the people passing below, a light breeze in her hair. She listened to the sound of music coming from deeper in the city's heart, carrying on the wind.

She was growing tired, but she didn't want to sleep. Instead she drank a glass of water in the kitchen, then poured a glass of the wine left over from the day before. She could see the light-filled window of the apartment across the road. A couple sat facing each other across a table set with white linen and limp, dying yellow flowers, maybe freesias. Her exhaustion had suddenly become unbearable. Outside, the sky was a profound and forgiving black. She staggered to the bed, and then there was nothing.

Return

Francis woke up from his deep sleep into the Monday that should have followed the last Sunday, and he was home, he recognized with gladness as he opened his eyes. And yet, already the memory of his anger was fading. Here he was, back in reality — time frozen, forgiven, the same way it had been before.

Real, he told himself as he showered with his usual soap, as he shaved, as he readied his things for work. I will be an advocate for what is real. Not hotel rooms, not slippery cities, not adventures. I've learned my lesson.

First he couldn't find his daughter's lunchbox, then she wouldn't eat the boiled egg his wife had made, and then she refused to get into the car. He had to bundle her up in his arms, making a game of it, almost throwing her in. I'm kidnapping you! he threatened, until she succumbed to laughter. In the morning's bustle he barely even noticed the strange wound on the back of his hand — reddened, weeping very slightly — until he saw his hands on the wheel.

What's that? asked his wife, noticing it too, leaning over from the passenger seat.

Nothing, he said, turning the key in the ignition.

Clara called in sick, took a Valium from Arturo's bedroom drawer and slept for most of the day, a scraped-out shell of time, hoping on each waking that she might open her eyes to elsewhere.

Francis performed the routines of his day – the packed lunch eaten in his office over a dog-eared paperback; the coaxing of panicked, surly graduate students; the crawl home through the traffic – with the gusto of a man who had returned from the dead.

It was wonderful to hold his daughter in his arms. He spent a long time putting her to bed, reading her three stories, stroking her hair until she protested.

Real, he repeated over and over to himself, as he and his wife sat at the dinner table, as he watched her teeth take on a blue tinge from the meal's wine, as he listened to her brush this tinge away afterwards while he sat in the marital bed, in his marital pyjamas.

He made himself come, quickly, quietly, when it was his turn in the bathroom, thinking about the smooth line of Clara's back, her collarbone, the soft skin of her hips. Even her small and unpretty feet, the soles of which were always somehow a little dirty – *sluttish*, he thought, involuntarily, religiously, right at the crucial moment. He let his breath out, took a moment to gather himself. Tears in his eyes. He opened the door back to the bedroom where his wife sat reading, neatly in place.

Real.

On Tuesday they both woke up, again, in the real world. Clara walked under rolling clouds to her job at the front desk of the gallery, and sat there silently. Young people dressed in black came in to look, nonplussed, at the sculptures of animals showing that month: chimeras of polystyrene and wire, painted with neon. They were ugly, she thought. Everything in the world was ugly.

She replayed Francis's words to her over and over. Yes, he had been cruel. But also, yes, she *was* selfish. Yes, she was childlike. He had seen through her so cleanly, so mercilessly. She cringed to think of how she had cried in front of him. How quickly she had ruined it all.

By Wednesday, Francis was agitated as he made his way across the city to the leafy grounds of the university, cycling to clear his head. He missed Clara. Once he admitted that he missed her – her warm body next to him first thing in the morning, yes, but her easy laugh too, her enthusiasm, her dedication to the cause of love as organizing principle – there was no going back. By Friday, it felt unbearable without her. How quickly it had happened. He felt disgusted at how he had hurt her wilfully and willingly, and for what?

Well, for the upholding of the family unit. No cause more noble. *Except, maybe, true love?* his conscience suggested then, undermining him – unfairly, he felt.

The carpet as grass. The tasteful lamps as sunsets. The bed as their home. The door as threshold impassable.

What if I never see him again? Clara thought, in terror.

It was entirely plausible.

Tense at the kitchen counter, she checked her phone for any messages from him, but nobody had messaged her at all. Then she went to read their old messages – she would just look, she promised herself, wouldn't contact him first, would never break that rule – but when she typed his name into the search bar, nothing came up. Not even a saved number. Had she deleted it accidentally? Or wiped him from her phone in an impulsive, sedated or drunken moment? She checked frantically, again and again. It had all vanished.

On the Saturday, Arturo insisted that he and Clara leave the apartment and go for a drink. He was the only person who knew about Francis, though he had never met him. Their city was too small. Francis's life was too precious.

In their favourite dark bar, they spoke fervently of the crises happening in Arturo's life – an errant romance, difficulties at work, the impossibility of decisions past, present and future – but when asked about her life, she found she could not discuss it. How could she explain? He had not noticed her absence in the apartment. It felt like a betrayal, though there had been no absence to notice. When she started to cry, yet again, he embraced her with a wordless, fierce hug. They paid up and walked home, Arturo cheerful and loping in his long grey coat, Clara bloodless, a burden, just past too drunk. The incessant crying was exhausting for her, for everybody around her, she knew. She swore she had not wept like this before she had met Francis. He had unpeeled the skin from her bones, had left her tender and exposed to the world, but that was also part of the appeal. To be closer to its wet and beating heart.

From her bedroom, Clara thought: *I would do anything to return.*
　　From his house, Francis thought: *I would do anything to return.*

And finally, on the Sunday, they found themselves once more in the apartment.

The Party

They woke at the same time – naked, stunned, as if thrown into the bed. Clara felt herself gathered desperately into Francis's arms. He kissed the top of her head over and over, her hair dampening with his tears. She could not move.

I'm sorry, he said, again and again. I was so hurtful.

She wanted to push him away, to be angry, but she couldn't. Her body fitted inside his embrace too perfectly. She manoeuvred so that they were face to face. His eyes were wild, cheeks red. She kissed his mouth.

It's all right, she said.

No, it isn't, he said.

It is, it is, she insisted.

He wrapped his arms around her even tighter. Oh my God, I missed you. I missed you so much, Clara.

She nestled her face into the warm dip of his chest and breathed in the scent of his sleep-sweet skin, so unmistakably him. It dizzied her, after their separation. How could she ever get used to being apart from him?

She asked him for a glass of water, and he got up at once. As soon as he was out of the bed and through the door she felt the urge to call his name, needlessly; just to feel the shapes of the syllables in her mouth, to transmit them from one room to another.

*

When they went outside that day, the city had changed. It was colder, for one thing, and the unmoving sky was greyer too, patterned with repetitive, teeming clouds that presumably threatened rain. Their favourite cafe in the square had vanished, replaced with a different one. This one had yellow chairs, a chequered yellow awning that had seen better days. They sat inside, at a table in the window, watching other couples pass. Clara tapped her teaspoon softly against the table.

It's different, she said.

It's still ours, Francis said.

It changes when we leave, she said helplessly. But I don't know what makes us leave. Or what brings us back.

Did anybody notice you had gone? Francis asked.

Nobody, she said. No time had passed.

Francis paused. He looked up to the sky, seemed to consider something.

Did you do anything differently last week? he asked.

No, she said. I went to work. I came home. Nothing happened, and nothing changed.

Same here, he said.

I missed you, she said. Even though you were cruel to me.

I missed you too, he said.

I *longed* for you, even, she said. I'd forgotten what that was like. This place has spoiled me.

She felt vulnerable, took a long drink of her suddenly cold coffee to disguise it.

You don't need to long for me, he said. I'm right here.

He looked tired.

Now we're back, we should stay alert, he said. Pay attention to things.

Clara nodded, silent.

But I think we should enjoy it too. Let's just have fun and be good to each other.

I'm always good to you, said Clara.

Let's be better, he said.

Don't say I'm like a child, then, she said.

Don't call me a middle-aged suburban father, he said.

But you are, she said, both of them starting to laugh.

I am, he said.

Not *suburban* though, Clara said, comfortingly. You're actually quite metropolitan. And youngish, even.

Thanks, said Francis.

Their laughter quietened.

I'm going to do my best, Clara, he said, serious now. Be patient with me.

Clara felt terrible.

Of course, she said. Of course.

The summer before they woke up in the city of impermanence, Clara had experienced a period of solitude. The gallery closed, the real city emptied in its most sweltering month, she found herself elsewhere. Another country, a sublet of a friend of a friend, the rooms sparse and shaded. Total freedom, she told herself doubtfully.

She found herself on hot, cobbled streets, turning her face up to sunlight. She found herself in cool churches, watching coloured light spill over stone. She found herself sitting at small tables, drinking small cold drinks from glass bottles. She found herself in a hotel room with a man, younger than her, with large sad eyes who watched her as she sat on the edge of his bed. She tried to explain to him that she was in love with someone who she mainly saw in hotels, and so to her the space was not just luxury, or holiday, but representative of a kind of neutral zone where they could be themselves together, where all was permitted, and then she asked if she could use his shower and cried, secretly, as she washed her body carefully with the hotel soap. In his body, laid out for her on the bed, she tried to simultaneously call up Francis's body and cast it away. What if sex was nothing but a repeatable trick, she thought; something that you could find an analogue for, another body to replace the beloved body, the desired object? It became her project of the summer. It did not feel like betrayal.

She rode the metro out of the city where she was living and held her head between her knees, rocking with nausea, then walked through scrubby woods to a blue lake where she could sunbathe naked. Strong gin and tonics in plastic glasses; men walking too close to her towel to look at her. A man about Francis's age tried to pick her up in a language that was not her own. She turned him down, but she was tempted, albeit tinged with repulsion. Repulsion did enter her physical repertoire, that summer. She was out of the habit of saying no. She wanted to say yes because she didn't know where the word would take her, because it still had possibility. But nobody was him, nobody could even come close.

Every day she spoke to Francis, sending long emails that he would reply to and then immediately delete. She told him about the water-rats swimming in the river, about cycling up that same river to tiny hamlets where she drank local beer and weaved her way unsteadily home, sent him photographs of churches, her sunburn, whitewashed buildings, castles. She told him about her meals as she ate them, wishing he were there. Fried cheese, gamey meats. Dumplings, scoops of ice cream the size of her fists, pastries. Some days she ate nothing, and some days she drank so much beer that she was sick; she did not tell him this. He received the curated version of her experience, the way he always had. It didn't feel like betrayal. Cherry vodka. Beef carpaccio. *Keep it together*, she thought as she walked around. In an art museum she watched a class of schoolchildren copy the paintings, jealously guarding their sketchbooks with their bodies. She watched the wasps swarm the fallen fruit in the park. She told him about all the bells in all the churches ringing out synchronized across her favourite hill, lushly verdant, at 6 p.m. He was there with her, he was always with her, except when it came to the bodies.

There were nights when she would press her face into her duvet and wring it between her fists and howl. She was alone. She could feel the fissures of her heart hardening, webbing. She was alone and she was happy and she was destroyed, for loving Francis meant that she would never love any other, she could see that clearly all those hundreds of miles away from him. He was in a different city, with a family that already loved him. At a party where she knew nobody an American girl pressed a tab of acid to her tongue, and then for twelve hours the city was unfamiliar. Around her it rained molten golden metal. The buildings quivered and her own eyes became larger, smaller, larger, when she looked in the mirror. She took a bubble bath with a carton of chocolate milk and stroked the skin of her legs through the blanket of foam, forgave herself every bad thing she had ever done, forgot this forgiveness when the sun came up and she was still awake. No matter. The city had a brittle sugar skin on it that day, when the acid had mostly worn off. The remembrance of wonder remained, the way it did in the days after she had seen Francis, when things glowed. She walked around a city made new the way that love made her walk around a city made new, dazed.

I want us to take a holiday, she told Francis. *Will we ever manage a holiday?*

Somehow we will manage it, he wrote back to her. *One day we will go somewhere hot and arid. I will drive. You will pick the music. We will stop to marvel at the rapeseed in the field, at the tiny ruins set into the hilltops, at the sea where it hits the horizon in a gleaming thread of blue. We will kiss carelessly in plazas, squares, restaurants, we will eat olives and spit the stones into small bowls, we will wake up hungover and dehydrated, our bodies slick with sweat. All of this is still ahead of us, it's incomprehensible that it will never happen at all.*

She read his email on a bench in a patch of shade, under a plum tree. She closed her eyes and let the warm air wash over her. Her concerns seemed paltry, suddenly.

And so her belief was renewed.

They went into a clothes shop to buy Clara one of the short dresses of pale yellow lacework that were fashionable there at the time. She took a long time trying it on, Francis waiting beyond the curtain, bored.

Where are you from? he asked one of the two assistants hovering nearby.

Paris, she said, gesturing to the laconic man at the till. They were tall as models and both dressed in plain, loose black.

And what do you call *this* city? he asked.

She looked at him as if he were stupid. We don't call it anything, she said.

Doesn't every city have a name? he asked.

I don't know, she said, shrugging. Her long, dirty-blonde hair fell over her face.

Clara came out with the dress over her arm, handing it to the man to fold deftly in layers of cloudy tissue paper. The price would take every coin that Francis and Clara had left between them, but they didn't hesitate, for they were reckless and in love and deserved beautiful things.

But when it came to paying the bill at a bar in the square later on, an afternoon bottle of crisp white wine drunk in the sun, Clara's purse and Francis's wallet were both empty. A dark-haired waitress tapped her foot, looked over towards her partner. She had seen this before.

First time's forgiven, she said. Second time isn't. Wait here a moment.

She went inside and came back with a newspaper, the same one Francis had discovered on the first day. This time the headline read *Breaking News: You Deserve to be Happy!* The waitress flipped it open to a section of job adverts which Francis hadn't seen before.

Plenty to choose from, she said, turning away to serve another table.

Together they studied the adverts. Each one listed two positions to be filled and stipulated joint application. Accountant and clerk. Waiter and waiter. Head chef and sous-chef. Clara put her finger to one: *Two gardeners wanted to tend the boating park.*

How about this? she said. Something outdoors.

She was not a gardener but had always liked the idea of being someone who might take it up in some vague, untethered edition of the future. She felt strongly, instinctively, drawn to the romantic idea of kneeling in the city's soil, of pruning leaves and keeping things beautiful. It was her face, illuminated, that convinced Francis, rather than the idea of getting his hands dirty all day.

It does seem to be our best option, he said.

He felt petulant at the idea that they had to work at all and saw no reason why they should be forced to, but there was no denying the empty wallet and so he went reluctantly inside with the newspaper and used the large yellow rotary telephone by the till to call the number listed. The waitress watched him. Francis smiled at her, and she smiled back. She was very pretty, he thought, then caught himself and turned away.

The man who answered the phone had a deep voice and a casual manner. He would be happy to have them, he said. They could start the next day and would work four days a week. That would be enough. He didn't ask about previous experience, previous jobs, or even if they had ever gardened before. It was very easy. Francis felt a sudden awareness of unreality – a bubble-like feeling, as if he were moving outside of his own body – which receded as quickly as it occurred.

When he hung up and turned around, the waitress was still watching him. He gave her a thumbs up and then regretted it.

Thanks, he said.

Not a problem, she said softly.

Francis walked out into the sunlight. Clara stood up as he approached.

The holiday's over, he told her.

Which meant, he supposed – he thought to himself with a sense of anticipation as they walked – that a kind of new life was truly beginning.

Clara woke before Francis the next day and watched him sleep, noting the sweetness of his face in repose. She saw vulnerability in him for the first time, as she watched. It unsettled her.

As they ate their overdone toast quickly, distracted by the prospect of their first day at work, she pictured him as he was in the museum. Recalling him as a beautiful, unknown object returned her to that time when he seemed to represent a vast and mysterious life, one out of her reach. Her own life had always been so knowable, and so accommodating. It had been waiting for him, leaving space the way one might leave a door ajar.

*

In a small building near the entrance to the park they found two bright green aprons, with secateurs and gloves and trowels in a brown leather bag each. There was another couple already there tending to the roses, a young blonde man and a tall, older woman. Two women in boilersuits, one blue and one red, pushed lawnmowers side by side on the grass. It was peaceful. Underneath the trowels there were white paper bags full of seeds labelled *Plant Me.* They walked outside and the four others paused briefly to greet Clara and Francis, waving from a distance, before returning to their tasks. Bags of damp, dark compost leaned against the building's wall. Francis took one, and they carried it to a bare flower bed, the tall woman pausing again to point them, wordlessly, in the right direction.

And this is how it would be. Clara put on the apron and gloves and then lowered herself, the grass still wet under her bare legs. She tipped out some of the seeds on to the palm of her gloves. They were bright red and shining; she had no idea what they were, and the packet gave no clue. No instructions. With the trowel, she took some compost and laid it, carefully, on top of the dry earth that lay there already. Francis knelt to join her. He showed her how to make indents in the compost with her fingers, gently, placing a seed in each one. It smelled of rain, though the sky was clear. He covered the seeds she had placed. She turned to look at him. He kissed her on the cheek, almost bashful. Would the city let them stay long enough to see the flowers grow? she wondered. It was possible they had already outstayed their welcome, that today like so many days could be their last.

After work, they stopped by the yellow cafe on the square. Francis opened the small cloth bag of gold that he had been handed as they left the park. Nothing extravagant, but they'd live. It was enough for coffee, for wine, for simple meals.

Privately, watching Francis as he counted out the coins, Clara admitted to herself that she missed the city of their first and second visits. She shivered slightly in a hard breeze. It was sunny again, but not quite warm. There was a cigarette burn on the table, and a crisp packet had blown underneath it. What had happened to that more perfect version? she thought with nostalgia. Be good, she told herself then. The main thing is that he is here with you. And yes, there Francis was, all trace of his earlier vulnerability gone, beautiful as ever, leaning back in his chair, his black T-shirt crumpled from the day. She could see the earth underneath his fingernails, the evidence of work they had done together. There were always new intimacies to be thrilled by. They did not need a city of unrelenting sunlight, of glittering fountains. It was better to live here, she thought, as she took a mouthful of coffee, where he was the shining thing who made all else fall into place. That was who he had always been to her. That was who he was.

Walking home, they saw that the gutters of the pavements were dirtier, the tarmac of the road pitted. Later in the week, they would realize, reluctantly, that even the milk they had bought from Paula and Jean soured faster in the fridge. The apartment was dingier too, the floors uneven. But they did not discuss this with each other. It seemed somehow disloyal to notice it, let alone to articulate it. The important thing was that they were there. Nothing else mattered if they were together.

Instead, Clara adjusted her expectations. Her joy was nuanced, capacious: there was still much to be found, much to be delighted in, much to be tended to. And so she cleaned in furtive, quick bursts, when Francis wasn't looking. She dusted the corners, arranged things nicely, so you couldn't see any patches of damp or wear. She was *making a home* for them, she thought in stunned, devout incredulity. She was making something real.

It had taken them a while to say *I love you*, in the real world. For a time, their names acted as proxies for the phrase. A name was both intimate and informative. The intimacy was achieved by context that could only really be experienced in the moment, and not kept as evidence to be used against them. *Clara, Francis, Clara, Francis,* swapped back and forth, until their names felt different altogether, because they meant *love*, and they also meant *love* could not be said.

Francis was a careful person, Clara less so. The careful person drives the declarations. Clara knew this, reminded herself of it when she became despondent of *I love you*'s lack. But Francis knew that, in the absence of concrete proof, in the absence of concrete life, *I love you* would take on an outsized weight. It would not simply be an expression of affection but would be seized upon with religious fervour by them both. An incantation, a binding, a promise. Without *I love you* there still existed a plausible deniability, a slipperiness in the contours of their relationship's topography. Sometimes they did not see each other for weeks, or even a month, without discussing it. Or without Francis discussing it; Clara was at the mercy of his schedule and cues, his whims, though he would not have thought of them like that. He would never admit it, but he did sometimes forget about her, though always briefly. Real life could be very pressing. He had occasionally wished for simpler times. Then he would un-wish this, and return to Clara without having technically left at all, without the absence being registered, and it was easy because her devotion forgave every bad thing he could do to it.

The word was finally broached on Clara's bed, in the apartment she had just moved into with Arturo. Almost eight months had passed since that first day in the museum. Nothing else was unpacked. They were alone. Francis brought her a bunch of pale yellow freesias and a postcard of *Still Life with Cherries and Mouse*, which she immediately tacked to the bedroom's bare wall. Together they pushed the bed to the centre of the room, boxes stacked around the walls. Together they made this bed, their hands quick and shaking with desire. Then they laid their bodies upon it. There were no curtains. The afternoon light was everywhere, made radiant all it touched. *I love you, Clara*, Francis said as they moved. Afterwards, they were still. The birds outside were singing.

From their living room one night they watched a party taking place in the apartment across the road, illuminated through the window. Three couples gathered around a long table, and when a man in a grey suit noticed Clara and Francis watching he waved, and Clara and Francis waved in response, and then everyone was waving and laughing. A tall woman in a burgundy dress beckoned them over. Within seconds the others were beckoning too, their arms moving exaggeratedly.

Oh, let's go and say hello, Clara begged. We've never been to a party together.

They found a bottle of wine in the fridge as if it had been waiting for the occasion, left the apartment and walked down the stairs, crossed the road. In the lobby of the other building, in low warm light, the woman in the burgundy dress was already waiting.

I'm Lili, she said. I'm so glad to meet you both.

She swayed up the stairs, quite drunk. And why shouldn't she be? thought Clara, who was also a little drunk, following her, feeling Francis's hand on the small of her back through the new dress they had bought together.

Although the apartment building seemed identical from the outside to Clara and Francis's own, inside it was more modern. Less tasteful, they both thought privately, though

Clara was impressed, despite herself. There was a cream leather sofa, a solid black marble coffee table. Geometric paintings on the wall. Another woman, and four men, awaited them. The women absorbed Clara at once, spun her to the other side of the room, taking the bottle of wine and complimenting her shoes. The men shook Francis's hand and introduced themselves one by one. Adan, Ellis, Max, Hans. They were handsome and well dressed, in black vests or white silk shirts and sharp tailoring, and the cocktail Adan poured was something with whiskey that tasted expensive when he sipped it.

Welcome to the city! exclaimed Adan, lifting up his glass. And how are you finding it?

It's wonderful, said Francis, knocking his cut-glass tumbler against Adan's. How about you?

It's fantastic, isn't it? Not to say we haven't had our challenges – here he motioned his head towards Lili, who was laughing with the other women – but it's really all worth it. More than worth it.

How long have you two been together? asked Max, wearing a dark grey suit and thick-rimmed glasses.

Eighteen months, said Francis. He swirled the drink around. The men nodded. And you?

We've been together almost a decade, me and Lil, said Adan.

An old-timer, said Ellis.

Not a devotional, though, said Hans.

Fuck those guys, said Adan.

Francis felt as if he'd lost a crucial thread. He tried to get back on track.

How long have you been coming here? he asked, addressing all of them.

Hans and Ellis were fair-haired and younger than the

rest. Ellis looked at Hans, then to the others. About a year, he said.

Max looked over towards the other woman with Lili and Clara – considerably older than him and sleekly silver-haired, in a black shift.

Me and Lena have been here a little less, he said. Nine, ten months, perhaps.

We've been lucky, said Adan. We never stay away too long. And these days we don't go away that often, either.

They've got it all figured out, said Max, nudging Adan.

Francis nodded, feeling overwhelmed. Do you have these parties often?

Oh yes, said Adan. It's our regular narcissists' convention.

I actually prefer the term *hopeless romantic*, said Ellis.

Whereas I favour *brooding philanderer*, said Max.

Classic, said Hans.

But with a heart, clarified Max.

I think *hopeless romantic* has that subtype covered, said Hans.

Not enough nuance, said Max, finishing his drink. Never enough!

We have Max to blame for the dramatic headlines in the paper, Hans said, turning to Francis. In the other place he's an ad man.

For my sins, said Max. What do you do, Francis?

I'm a professor, replied Francis.

Of what? asked Ellis, interested suddenly.

Art history, he offered, feeling strangely foolish.

Now, that's romantic, said Max. Was she your student?

What? No, said Francis, mildly appalled.

Seminars full of swooning girls, I bet, said Max. Love notes in the cubbyholes. Good-looking chap like you.

Stop scaring him, said Adan.

I'm a lawyer, said Ellis. But I've always wanted to be an artist, always really felt myself as one.

Ah, my wife's a lawyer, said Francis, before he could stop himself.

There was a sudden hush, as clean as if it were coordinated. For a moment, none of the men could meet his eye.

Sorry, he said.

Happens to the best of us, said Hans. Force of habit.

It never happened, said Max, making a zipping motion across his lips.

I'm glad that you met us, said Adan, making intense, meaningful eye contact with Francis. It's good to be around people who *get* it. You know? He put a hand on his shoulder.

When was the last time you told anyone in the other place about you two? he continued, gesturing over at Clara.

Well, I've never told anyone, said Francis. At that he felt a little pathetic.

Now, that's discipline, said Ellis.

I could never talk to anyone about it either, said Max, supportively. What were they going to say? Well done, and go off and enjoy yourself?

It's all about shame, said Adan. They're obsessed with shame over there.

It's actually very brave to live the way we do, said Max.

Ellis put his arm around Hans.

Clara was in the bathroom with Lili, watching her as she cut a blue powder into lines with a razor blade on a white porcelain plate. Lili lowered her head and sniffed, gracefully, through a metal implement. She lifted her head and shook her black curls before turning to the mirror and reapplying her lipstick, the same colour as her dress.

Clara took her turn with the implement, threw her head back. She watched Lili through the dissipating stars of her vision.

I think I love you, Clara said to her.

Lili smiled but didn't say anything. She was a shark, Clara thought, unbothered by this assessment, hoisting herself up on to the countertop, the same solid marble as the living-room table. The bathroom was bigger than theirs, plusher. Lili put the lipstick down and observed her.

Tell me, Clara, are you an idiot?

Pretty much, said Clara.

I knew you would be fun, said Lili.

I can be.

Francis must enjoy that. He seems serious.

He's just a little reserved with new people, said Clara.

Actually she had no idea if this was true, she realized. No matter. She felt a warmth as the mysterious drug took hold. Lili noted how she closed her eyes briefly, in bliss, giving herself over to it completely.

You didn't even ask me what it was, she said, indicating the plate with her head. Clara opened her eyes lazily.

I trust you, she said, closing them again. It would be rude of you to drug me unconscious in the bathroom the first time we met.

You're at a gathering of totally morally upstanding people, as you know, Lili replied.

They both started to giggle together, guiltily. Clara swung her legs. Her skin prickled. It was all so new, so pleasant.

We've never been to a party together before, she said. Can you believe it?

I can believe it, said Lili. I remember our first party. I was so happy that I drank until I was sick. I was spinning around the lamp posts.

She put both her hands on Clara's face, unexpectedly, and looked at her closely. Clara was disconcerted by the fine lines around Lili's dark eyes at close range, the aniseed of her breath.

You're a lone wolf. I can see it written all over you. Do you really love him? Lili asked.

More than anything, said Clara, unsettled, but without hesitation.

Lili released her, impressed.

Then be good, she said, turning back to the mirror, checking her nostrils for traces of blue.

What do you mean? asked Clara.

Lili didn't move to look at her. You know, she said. The threshold.

I don't know anything. Tell me, Clara said, with such urgency that Lili paused. She turned to consider Clara's imploring face for a long moment.

Of course, she said. You're new here. You've just been shuttling back and forth with no idea.

Yes, said Clara.

It's scary at first, isn't it? said Lili.

Do you get used to it?

Yes, I think you do, once you understand it more, said Lili.

She paused again.

It's about hurting your other – doing them harm. You're not supposed to hurt each other here, not seriously. Obviously hurting each other a little is unavoidable, we're only human. But there's a threshold of harm that's allowed, and once you cross this threshold you're *both* sent back.

She clapped her hands.

Spat right back into the big, bad, real world! she announced. And left there for however long. We haven't worked out how to come back yet. But we pine and we pine and we miss each other, and we keep the fire burning. And maybe it's just a matter of waiting, of loving, because eventually we wake up back here, and the counter's reset somehow.

Clara looked at her in astonishment.

That's all I know, said Lili. She gestured to the bathroom door, to the voices outside it. A few of us, those who arrived around the same time, put our heads together and figured it out. It took an experiment or two.

Clara nodded slowly.

How much harm is allowed? she asked.

Lili shrugged. It's trial and error, unfortunately. You'll probably get a sense for it. But you know when you've crossed the threshold, because of these.

She proffered her wrist, neatly bandaged, a spot of blood showing through.

The city leaves a mark, she said. A wound.

Clara pointed, questioning, at her ankle, where her own wound had healed in a neat circle, still red.

Lili nodded, turned to leave. So be good, Clara. That's all you can really do. Unless you want to go, of course. She hesitated before she opened the door. Or he does.

When Clara entered the living room, Francis was sitting on the cream leather sofa next to Adan. She compared the lean lines of his body to Adan's more compact build, the quiet vitality of how Francis moved his hands while he talked next to Adan's relative stillness; and to see Francis's body at long range, interacting in a way she rarely saw it, sheened it with novelty. She wondered how it would feel to watch him dance, or jump, or sprint. There were so many movements and actions that she had still never seen. Then there was pleasure too in the walk across the room, getting nearer and nearer to them, the subsequent sitting down and curling her body into Francis's. Here, in this room, he was hers.

And yet. *Lone wolf*, she thought later, back in the bathroom but without the blue powder, without Lili's perfumed hands on her face. Unsteady, taking a moment. She felt paranoid suddenly, splashed her face with cold water, then drank directly from the tap, mouth almost kissing the metal. A surge of muffled laughter from the others through the door. It was true. She was an only child who no longer spoke to her parents, who had left home, cut every tie, as soon as she was able to. She spoke to nobody of this, not even Arturo, not even Francis. And she had been alone, mostly, and she had been free, but then she had spent the last eighteen months in complete submission to this love. So did this mean she had squandered her freedom? she wondered. Or was she still free? She didn't feel so.

They were quiet as they returned home, crossing the dark street, no stars in the sky. Just the flash of cold night and then in, the clatter of Clara's heels on the tiles of the lobby, holding on to the banister, Francis walking ahead of her. He seemed removed from her, a remove that reminded her of their first day in the city, that reminded her also of the real city. How he vanished, was always vanishing, without warning. Sudden terror. She wanted to pull him to the ground.

I didn't like those people, Francis said when they were back in the apartment, putting the kettle on.

They seemed fine, said Clara, falling into a chair. Ten years together, can you imagine? I wonder why they're not together in the real world.

I suppose the same reasons we're not, said Francis, who had been with his wife for twelve. He passed her a cup of tea.

Remind me of those reasons again, she said as she took it, shaking just a little.

Clara, he said, putting his hand to the back of his neck and looking away. Let's not do this now.

He seemed tired rather than angry, but she backed down regardless. She didn't have the energy for it either.

Would you fuck Lili? she asked instead.

Oh, probably, he said. I wouldn't dare turn her down. I wonder what happens if you sleep with someone else here?

Factory reset, said Clara. Total apocalypse meltdown.

Maybe there are orgies happening all over the city, he said. We should have asked them.

You'd love that, she said, taking a sip of her tea.

Mostly I wouldn't know what to do with myself.

I'd show you.

I know you would.

In the bedroom they stood on opposite sides of the bed and took off their clothes, watching each other. Clara felt combative, wary. But when they lay down, it was Francis who pulled her towards his body more violently than usual. He bit her shoulder and so she bit his in return, sharply, in surprise. She dug her nails into his back – asserting herself or punishing him, she wasn't sure. Those things allowed to be done to her, normally strictly forbidden to be done to him. But there was no protest. She tightened her grip. So did he. Leave something real on me, Clara begged silently, the way she had done so many times before. Leave me something to remember you by.

Francis dropped off to sleep first, as Clara was learning he usually did – sleep's onset preceded by a sharp inhale, as she had also learned. She sat up and watched Francis as he slept, a strip of moonlight over his face.

For hadn't she always waited, and always returned? Hadn't her devotion forgiven every bad thing that could be done to it?

He slept so soundly, as if he had not a care in the world.

It struck her with an irresistible, terrible force: she could leave, if she wanted to. If she was prepared to inflict harm, she could be the one who left.

When the last thing happens, you don't always know it's the last thing. The last time to wake up together, or go to sleep, the last meal or kiss or platitude. But when they had been in the real city, Clara and Francis had lived under the assumption that every action was plausibly the last between them. Each beautiful moment evaporated like water on hot earth, so that every kiss became a kind of pre-emptive mourning, and so that every kiss — hoped for, dreamed of, never taken as their right — also became a bounty, a miracle. Each hotel room, each short afternoon in Clara's apartment, was a page drawn upon and then discarded, leaving the page after it blank, as if the one before had never happened.

You must think carefully about this love, Arturo had told Clara, before. She was crying in their bathtub after her birthday party, which Francis had missed. Everyone else was gone. Eight inches of too-hot water, lavender bubble bath, and Arturo sitting on the floor next to the tub. Lucid light of dawn.

Do you know what I'm saying? said Arturo, leaning over to turn on the cold tap. Clara writhed as the water hit her bare skin. Do you understand me?

Yes, she said.

He's not the person you believe him to be, he said.

You wouldn't think that if you met him, said Clara.

Then let me meet him, he said.

Clara was silent. Arturo sighed.

I'll wash your hair, he said.

She nodded obediently. He shifted around, told her to lean back, rinsed her scalp with hot water from the shower head. Clara felt her hair grow heavy.

I love him, Clara said. I don't know what to do.

Arturo considered this as he massaged her scalp. His fingers were gentle.

You should leave him, he said eventually. You already know this.

But even at the thought of that Clara felt her body tense.

I can't bear it, she said. I can't think of my life without him.

Arturo sighed.

You need to see it through, then, he said. I won't stop you, even though I love you.

It's because you love me that you won't stop me, said Clara.

She turned around and pressed her wet forehead against his dry one. Together they stayed like that for a moment.

Clara, lying next to Francis, thought about a threshold, stretched out like an electric wire – something you crossed over, somewhere you crossed into. A line you inched closer to, until it was too late.

Francis seemed to rouse briefly, turning over in his sleep and slinging an arm across her. His face pressed into her shoulder.

How old is your daughter now? she said aloud.

He stiffened and withdrew at once, awake suddenly, or

perhaps he had been pretending all along. Rolling on to his back, he looked up at the ceiling. He was silent for a long time.

Four, he said, in the end. My daughter is four years old. Elise.

Clara stared at the ceiling too. In the corner of the room, a new crack was spreading out against the plaster.

Morning coffee, their usual table. Clara was fractious, hungover. Francis seemed uncertain how to handle her. He wasn't holding himself with the same authority as usual, and she felt a kind of exasperation, even a scorn. *Middle-aged father*, she thought. *Beloved object*, she thought then, involuntarily loyal. She crumbled the stale biscuit that came with her coffee into a pile of crumbs, scattered by the wind. The sky was a smooth and universal grey that you would never see in the real world. It wasn't even trying, she thought. She pictured men on long ladders at night, carelessly pasting rolls of sludge-coloured paper over the lovely sky of the day before.

She made a show of looking in her bag. I need cigarettes, she said to Francis, looking up. I feel like one. I won't be long.

All right, he said, brow furrowed. He reached across and took her hand, but she snatched it back. He looked up at her, hurt, but she wouldn't meet his eyes.

She walked quickly, out of the square and into the dark and shaded streets where others strolled hand in hand. It felt furtive, being alone. The nausea, the sense of an elastic stretching, came on at once. She breathed through it – one long breath, two. It was telling her not to stray too far from him, she understood by now. But she kept walking. By the window of a gift shop, she steadied herself by studying embroidered handkerchiefs, kitsch blouses with lacework at the collar and hem. Everything was so orderly, so false. She felt violent suddenly, it all made her feel so exposed, and she had the urge to smash the shop window, to find something and hurl it through the glass.

Francis, waiting, folded a pale blue paper napkin into quarters. The moment she was out of sight he felt unsure if she would return. He felt a tugging, anxious nausea in his chest, but also a faint trace of relief in the idea that he might be free of Clara at last, and then he felt terrible for even this hint of an idea, and he wanted to weep then, with remorse and with fear.

Clara walked on, uphill. Her shoes felt waterlogged, heavy, her body no longer obedient. But she knew, somewhere, that it was important to continue. To see how far she might make it. In a doorway she paused for a moment, knifed at the waist. Blood rushed to her head. Passing couples looked her over with interest, but said nothing.

Francis was crying openly, amazed by his own tears. The yellow freesias on the table in front of him were visibly browning, the petals falling. The pain at his chest was incredible.

It hurts, he wanted to tell someone, anyone, with the incredulity of a baby. It hurts!

Clara gulped for air, but she was obstinate, did not stop again, even though she knew it must be hurting Francis too, he who now seemed a long way away.

Francis raised the cup with shaking hands to his lips, spilling coffee over the table. A waitress came over with more napkins and cleaned it up, the coffee blooming on paper damply, like a cloud. Francis looked up at her but did not know how to ask for help. What would he say? *She's gone, and I don't know when she'll be back.* Already it seemed to him like the details of Clara were fading; he ran through a panicked inventory, *dark hair, freckles, loud laugh, wide mouth, blue dress, long legs,* but they were abstract qualities that swam around themselves, stubbornly refusing to cohere.

Clara arrived at a large flight of sandstone steps that she had not seen before, stretching so high she couldn't see what was at the top. She climbed up them until she felt too weary to carry on, still only halfway up. She sat for a moment. From the steps she could survey the city from an unfamiliar angle. It was peaceful at that time of day. Nobody else seemed in any kind of rush. Her heart felt ragged, manhandled. One of the stones of the steps was crumbling, a tiny purple flower growing from it. She plucked the flower and watched it shrivel immediately in her palm. She worried at the small hole in the stone, scraping at it with her fingernails until she broke off a small piece, and then a larger one. Out of nowhere a quick, sharp pain in the crook of her elbow. A small round wound. She breathed out – a long, defeated exhale.

When she returned to Francis, where he was still blotting at the coffee on the table, his cheeks were wet and he was breathing rapidly, though when she asked why, he could not explain.

She didn't tell him about the wound on her arm. She would keep the information to herself a little longer, she decided. Couples milled around the fountain, the water choked with gold.

*

Had she meant to cause him pain – to punish him, even? Or had it been a weak attempt to assert her independence? Pure thoughtlessness? Thinking back on it later, she couldn't understand why she had done it. Francis was solid in her arms, and she did not want to leave. She felt sure she would not sleep, but she did so easily.

Francis watched her, lying motionless. She was flushed, mouth pursed, and very still. He put his ear closer to her lips to check she was still breathing.

After an hour or so he got up and went to the bathroom. As he washed his hands, he studied the ring on his finger. It seemed ridiculous to be wearing it. He pulled at it, but it wouldn't move. His hands must have swollen. He pulled at it harder. He scooped a gouge in the bar of soap and rubbed it against the metal to loosen it, but still it would not move. He abandoned the task and returned to the bed, where he found, finally, that he could sleep after all.

Return

But it had been enough to cross the threshold, enough to push them across the invisible line separating world from world. And so they did wake apart, briefly, but it was a roiling, dreamlike awakening, unlike the ones before. Clara opened her eyes and glimpsed her home, her real home, in the darkness, and she was bereft even though she knew it was her fault, and then she closed her eyes and it slipped away. Francis swam up towards waking, but turned and slipped back into uneasy sleep, the real world more dream than the unreal. They touched the other life lightly and returned, almost at once.

Francis woke to the apartment dark and cold. Outside, heavy rain washed against the window. Clara was beside him, already awake. She reached out a hand to cup his face.

It's like being in a boat, she said.

They listened to the puling wind. Clara switched on the lamp beside the bed, a pool of hopeful light. She wrapped a blanket around herself, shivering, and went to the other room. The coffee, when she brought it back to Francis in bed, was burnt. They did not talk about their brief visit to the real world.

Clara collated the new things. The crack in the ceiling, already worsened. When she went to the bathroom some tiles had come loose, and the windows were seamed with black mould. She retreated to the bed, which remained a sanctuary. There they stayed, quiet, until the rain appeared to cease.

Outside, the cafes in the square were boarded up, broken glass scattered on the ground in front of one. They saw figures moving quickly on the far side of the square, surreptitiously, as if they were afraid to be outside. The fountain was dry except for pooled rainwater, plastic rubbish intermingling with the few remaining coins.

I've done this, thought Clara, with horror and with awe.

They walked further, seeking familiarity, and found the park where they worked smaller and muddier, the trees losing their leaves. Nobody was boating on the lake, and none of the other gardeners was present.

They walked on to the nearest metro station, City North, and they waited a long time under flickering, greenish lights for a train, but nothing came. They could hear only a rattling in the distance. When another couple walked down unsteadily into the station and stood on the other platform, staring at Francis and Clara with an uncomfortable intensity, they decided enough was enough.

Back at the apartment she asked Francis if he wanted wine, but he didn't, so she went alone to the fridge and poured herself a small glass, drank it fast like water in the blue light of the fridge even though it was sour, her throat bobbing. She poured another glass and took it to the sofa, sipped it as she watched Francis read the book about Flemish still lifes. She took the other book, the novel they both loved. Though she had read it several times, she opened it once more. Francis put his arm around her absent-mindedly.

The story was not how she remembered it, with more

unhappiness, and the wrong character names. She skipped ahead a few pages, then a few more, to find their fortunes only worsened. She read melodramatic conversations that felt transplanted from a different book. The narrator was falling to pieces. She closed the novel in disgust.

The rain became harder, the sky darker. The air was freezing. Clara fetched the throw from the bed, wrapping it around herself, and went to the window to watch the water falling, gathering, down in the street. She watched a couple sheltering across the road under a narrow lip of building, and imagined the water rising, higher and higher, until they were stuck in the apartment, as if on an island. The idea was not unpleasant.

It might flood, she said to Francis, turning back over her shoulder. He was struck by how the light of the window framed her. How she could be as beautiful and still as a portrait, when she wanted to be.

They went to the bed and lay clothed, close, their faces almost touching. They were silent for a long time.

I have to tell you something, she said. She took his hands in hers.

All right, he said evenly, heart cold.

This is my fault, she said.

I don't know what you mean, he said, confused, a little relieved.

I did this to the city, she said. I made it awful.

Clara explained what Lili had told her in the bathroom: the threshold of harm they should not step over, the spitting back into the real world, the uncertainty of return. Her eyes were wet.

I didn't mean to hurt you, she said. I just panicked. Something came over me.

I see, he said.
I feel terrible, she said.
You should have told me at once, he said.
She was fervent, febrile.
I'll never keep anything from you again, she said.

They lay there in silence for a while. Francis was thinking. He was angry at Clara, angry at the city. He tried not to show it. He could tell by her breathing that she was relieved to have confessed, that she was almost asleep, lulled by the storm. He kissed her forehead. He kissed her mouth. Her lips were chapped, her breath bad. She was becoming ordinary. It scared him a little to recognize this. The room was chilled.

What if we try to leave again, to leave properly? he said. And when we return, things might be better.

What do you mean? she murmured.

I mean, perhaps we have to make some kind of sacrifice to the city, he said.

She opened her eyes, considering this.

Hurt each other deliberately?

Yes, he said.

But what if it doesn't work, she said. What if it makes things worse?

He held her gaze.

It's a risk, he said. But we can't live in the city when it's like this, anyway.

The wind was higher. A branch, some piece of detritus, struck the window. Clara flinched.

We might not return at all, she said eventually, so softly it almost wasn't audible. The city might send us away for ever.

I don't think it will, Francis said. He felt a strange confidence in his plan, a sense that the city would reward the two of them working together, learning its rules, taking them seriously. He felt excited, even overcome, all at once.

Just miss me, he continued. Dream of me. Don't forget me. I'll do the same for you.

Clara laughed, a brief and bitter noise from deep in her throat.

I have longed to forget you, sometimes, she said. I have longed to know what my life might have been without you in it.

Francis was still.

But I can't, she said. And so I will wait to return.

How best to harm the other? He could have told Clara that she was right, that her boundless waiting made her pathetic. He could tell her about how he had longed to rip down the flimsy sky where it floated above them, to pull the flowers and turf of the city's parks up by the roots. He could tell her about how it had felt that day in the hospital when his daughter was born, a day Clara would never encroach upon or compete with. But there, on the bed, with her eyes locked on his like a wild animal, he found he did not have the appetite for those words, to weigh and portion what could be said without permanent damage.

Instead, by mutual agreement, they decided on physical harm. And so Clara went into the bathroom and returned with the blade of Francis's razor.

Francis went first, as she had hurt him the last time. It seemed only fair. He deliberated for a long time. Theoretical cruelty was different from the reality of Clara's body under his hands as he ran them along her. Her pale face that loved him, that trusted him so, swimming in the gloom.

He laid the blade against the soft skin of her thigh, just

above the knee. It was difficult to find the requisite force, and when he did Clara gasped, a thin line of blood springing up.

I can't, he said, horrified.

You have to, she said.

He made two more cuts swiftly, neatly. It became easier. He was readying for a fourth when she put her hands on his.

Enough, I think, she said. My turn.

Hovering above him in the dark, holding the blade, she felt vertiginous. Blood snaked down her leg, though she couldn't see it. He was so still that she wondered if he had fallen asleep. She knelt beside the bed. He looked up at the ceiling, at the widening crack. He felt her hands, delicate, pushing up his T-shirt. Her lips against the skin of his stomach. She laid her cheek against him, as if against a cool window. The sting as she pressed the razor lightly against his flank. Once, twice, three times. Francis held his breath, closed his eyes, sensed her leave and then returning. He felt a damp cloth against his skin. She held it there until the blood stopped. She had not cut deeply. Clara wondered briefly whether this kindness might absolve the cruelty, undo their work.

Then Francis felt a pain at the crook of his elbow. It was not from Clara's razor; he held out his arm to show her another of the strange round wounds, blood springing from its edges. Clara nodded. She pulled up the sleeve of her T-shirt to show him a corresponding wound, at the top of her arm.

So now we wait and see, she said.

Strange cost, strange warning, strange sign to prepare for exit.

They took off their clothes and lay together in the bed, pressed as closely to the other as they could manage. The rain stopped before they fell asleep.

They had slept together for the first time in an attic room she was briefly renting. All the other tenants were at work, the house quiet for once. A year behind her was the end of a long relationship with someone her own age. The relief of this relationship's final acts had rendered her clarified, newborn. Her life felt open.

Afterwards they had lain side by side on the small bed, close but somehow separated, not entwined in the way they would grow to rest afterwards in times to come. Francis's breathing was deep, reassuring. The cream paper lampshade was grimed at the seams with dust. Open the curtains, Francis told her, and when she did the room felt transformed. Afternoon light. She returned to the bed. He stared straight up, at the ceiling. His chest moved steadily up and down. She turned on her elbow to look at him and pressed one finger to his broad shoulder. He smiled, but didn't shift. She moved her lips to his shoulder, then nipped at his skin lightly with her teeth. This he reacted to, flinching.

Stop that, he said at once. You can't do that.

Clara pulled away, heart beating.

She had spent the morning before he arrived clicking through photographs of his wedding, a few years before. It had been easy to track him down. Afterwards their long honeymoon in remote and beautiful corners of Europe, oceans and rivers, villas set in the mountains. It seemed strange to her that his golden life could also contain moments like this: the listless afternoon room, the hard bed of a stranger, betraying his wife with someone whose last name he didn't yet know. She wanted to ask which was his real life, the goodness or the badness, but she didn't have the words to ask, and never really found the words to ask, or perhaps she simply came to know that there was no one *real* life, that everyone contained contradictions and falsehoods and secret places that others could not access.

His eyes closed, but he wasn't asleep.

Do you want something to eat? Clara asked, abashed. Or another drink?

I don't need anything, he said.

Without opening his eyes he moved his large and rough-knuckled hand to find hers, and held it, not unaffectionately.

Before leaving he showered in the bathroom quickly, furtively, with a bar of soap he produced from his bag. He discarded the packaging, and when he was gone Clara rifled through the bin for proof of what had taken place. She felt stupefied by what had filled the hours between his arrival and departure, how implausible it had felt. But here was the evidence. Three milky, clammy condoms, each tied in a knot. One empty bottle of wine. The soap's wrapper revealed that the one he used was a popular everyday brand, scented faintly with jasmine.

When she went into the bathroom, she saw he had left the soap itself behind. At the time she had been glad, thinking it meant intent to return soon, the way you might claim a new lover's bathroom with a toothbrush. But in the hotels they visited afterwards he did the same thing – produced the new bar of soap and discarded the packaging, left the soap behind every time — and she very quickly grew to understand that it was simply the soap he used at home, that all evidence must be erased upon the end of each meeting, so it was as if nothing had taken place. As if, when she was out of his sight, she did not exist at all. She tried not to think about how he had learned to do this. It was possible, she told herself, that he was just naturally cautious.

For their first couple of meetings Francis had discreetly removed his wedding ring, but Clara soon insisted she didn't mind. The risk of forgetting to put it on again, or losing it, was much greater, she argued. And while she encouraged him to wear the scent she loved, the one she sprayed on to cardboard tabs at the airport, she stopped wearing perfume around him, unprompted, to make the project of secrecy feel more collaborative. Together they whittled down risk after risk. He noticed, and thanked her. She was thrilled by his acknowledgement. They were not using the word back then, the word for which their names were proxies.

Clara never erased the evidence. She avoided showering afterwards for as long as she could manage, to keep the specific, indescribable scent of his skin on hers. Later, on the rare occasions he could be persuaded to visit the apartment she shared with Arturo, she wouldn't change the sheets afterwards until she absolutely had to. After that first time, she showered with the soap he left behind in the house-share until it wore down into a sliver. And then she was bereft. He had left her no other proof except for that.

Whenever she saw the same brand of soap in the supermarket she was immediately filled with longing, this soap that she had previously considered cheap and functional.

He never returned to that room again. But she didn't live there much longer, anyway.

*

After Clara had moved in with Arturo, she found herself encouraging him to travel – to visit his brother in Marseilles, to stay for the weekend with the rich poker player he had met at a hotel bar. To have adventures that would take him into the sprawling, glittering world, in order that she might, briefly, persuade Francis to retreat into her own compressed one.

And so one day Francis was lying on the sofa, incredibly, reading out loud to her. There was a hole in his sock, a glimpse of skin. It felt pornographic to witness. She wanted to sink to her knees.

She knew the secrecy was an aphrodisiac for him, whereas the most perverse act she could think of was walking down the street holding his hand.

And yet, secrecy demanded care. Secrecy demanded the building of a haven. Secrecy, in its own ways, quickly became domestic.

On one of the last afternoons before they discovered the city of impermanence, Clara sat in the window of a hotel, one they had visited before. The familiarity was reassuring. It was a kind of home. She was wearing a slip of black silk, but her legs and feet were bare. She curled them underneath her as she watched the streets of the city below.

Why can't we be together? she asked, but it was almost rhetorical, her eyes tracking the traffic.

We are together, said Francis.

You know what I mean, said Clara.

It wasn't the first time they had had this conversation. Francis sighed.

And *you* know I can't leave them, he said.

He did love her, and he did want to be with her. He dreamed of an erotic domesticity, Clara's face in the morning, meals and long walks. But he already had reality elsewhere, reality which he sometimes felt trapped by, he would admit, but which he could not truly imagine cutting loose.

Clara didn't push it.

Do you ever think about how, if we die, our entire world together disappears? she asked instead. Nobody else has ever been a part of it.

Francis nodded.

Until then, I will remember everything, he said. I'll remember enough for everyone.

But remembering is subjective, she said. Remembering isn't proof.

We don't need proof, he said.

Clara looked back out of the window.

Sometimes you're almost more real to me when we're apart, she said, after a long pause. I can call you up with such detail it's like you're actually there.

That's nice, he said.

But then I think, *When this ends, how will I ever get over it?* You'll still be in everything I do, she said, her tone neutral. I've memorized you so well.

Don't think about it ending, he said. Anyway, isn't there something romantic in the idea we'll leave nothing behind?

No trace, she said. Except for our secret objects.

The votives, he said. Those are for the future archaeologists. They'll be holding the most erotic button of all time. Except they'll have no idea what a precious discovery it is.

Poor them, she said, unfolding her legs, moving across the room to kiss him.

Another Sunday in the real world, this one entered smoothly. The eggs once more cracked by Francis into the pan, his daughter clinging to his knees. She seemed tearful, though he could have been imagining it. Was his wife more subdued than usual? He tried to catch her eye over the breakfast table and was stricken, for the first time, with extravagant guilt.

After breakfast he covered the thin cuts on his abdomen, and the wounds, with blue plasters patterned with dinosaurs.

Clara woke up. She opened her eyes but did not move. Wasn't the sun shining? She could hear her neighbour in the apartment next door playing the piano, imperfectly but with enthusiasm. These were not inconsequential joys. Francis still loved her, would be returned to her, if she kept believing. She only had to wait.

When Francis fucked his wife later that week he was present, respectful, but occasionally he would catch himself mid-movement and forget if it was something they had always done together or whether it was something Clara liked, and wondered if his wife felt that she was lying with a stranger, and to compensate he tried to devote himself to her pleasure rather than his own, until he felt her cool hands settle on his shoulders. It's all right, she said. It's all right. You can stop.

*

To be alone, Clara wondered, at the other end of the real city — was it really so bad? She did have almost total freedom, as Francis said. She could go where she wanted, do what she wanted. And she was never really alone anyway, with Francis so determinedly in her thoughts. There were many ways to love a person, she understood. The crisp air seemed full of possibility. Could both cities be reconciled, the limitations of each accepted? Was there a way to live like this?

She walked for miles across the real city after work one day, to re-establish herself within it. She felt like she had been away for years. Passing through the park by the university, she quickened her step, her eyes primed for Francis automatically. His number was still missing from her phone.

North to south along the canal. The sky was blue, then grey and spotting with rain, then blue again. By the time she met Arturo for dinner at their favourite Chinese restaurant, it was dark and her legs were aching.

You're pale, little ghostling, he said, backlit by strings of coloured lights. Eat some red meat or something.

She sipped her beer. She was happy to see him, had missed him, she realized. Of course, he hadn't missed her. The real city had been frozen, waiting for life to resume. She tried not to give herself away with too much affection.

How's ruining the heart of every eligible local bachelor going? she asked.

Brilliantly, he said. How's the married man of mystery?

Fine, she said, but refused to divulge any more information, protective of the city of impermanence, ever more precious at a distance.

Alone in the bathroom, late in the evening, Francis wept. He missed Clara. He missed something else too, something ineffable; not as gauche as the *self*, but perhaps some previous snapshot of it. A person who – impossibly – had been happy without her, who had been happy without knowing her.

Clara started to feel a new affection for the real city: its cheerful grime, the ebbing crowds of people, the stray cats wriggling in patches of sunlight, the bouquets of flowers stacked in black buckets outside the corner shops. She bought bunch after bunch of tulips, and they did not die, or at least not right away.

Still, every night before bed, she recited her litany with the patience of a true believer. She mouthed the words to the air, tried to transmit them from one city to the other.

I would do anything to return.

She moved from hope to restlessness to resignation, and then back, with arpeggio swiftness.

Francis cycled one evening past the museum where he had met Clara. They had been back there together just once, a few months before.

It was not raining that time, but a clear early-autumn day. Clara wore a long black dress that tied at the neck, her hair up, small silver hoops in her ears. When Francis arrived she was already there, and he stood behind her, the way he had done the first time. He took a step closer. She didn't turn around. She walked away, to the next painting, then the next room. He followed her. Tendrils of dark hair wrestled sweetly from her pins, told him that she had cut her hair shorter since he had last seen her. She always returned to him somewhat changed; he would never be able to fully grasp her, and yet this made him want to try harder, made him love each iteration anew. One day to look at her neck, to notice a haircut, might feel ordinary, and in that moment there would be both loss and implicit gain. When she had looked back over her shoulder at him, her smile seemed to hold the promise of everything good and easy in the world, and he felt all the unbearably beautiful moments of his life in his body, crowded as teeth in a mouth.

It had been his best year, he had thought there, suddenly overwhelmed. The only true year of his life.

As he pedalled furiously, Francis was struck by an urge to cast the bike away, to run into the museum and push past the guards, to wait for her in the endless rooms. He would pace, and plead, and stay for as long as it took. But it was late, and dark, and the museum was closed. And he knew she wouldn't be there, anyway.

In the long, silent hours behind the reception desk at the gallery, Clara started to draw. She drew what she could remember of the square with the fountain, the landscape of the beach and ring of water. She drew her own hand with her other hand, placing it on the desk. She tried to draw Francis from memory, but it was too difficult, too painful, his face eluded her. She drew the visitors in the gallery instead with quick, darting lines.

The day her period arrived in a surge of dark blood, a couple with a toddler came into the gallery. She watched the small child, a boy, walk unsteadily on the concrete floor. She held her breath in case he should fall, but he remained upright.

They hadn't taken any precautions in the other city. She knew that this was reckless, given all that had happened. And yet she also understood instinctively that nothing could grow in a body that was not really her body, a body hovering in a place that was really nowhere.

*

The days rolled on, then weeks; then a month, then another. It was possible that Francis had been too arrogant in thinking he could outwit the city of impermanence. He tried to stay very calm. He bargained with the weather. *If the rain stops in five minutes, I'll wake up there tomorrow.* He stepped over the cracks in the pavement with care. He kept the button from Clara's dress in his pocket at all times, touched it as often as he remembered.

I would do anything to return became a living prayer, larger than the world of him and Clara, a mournful incantation calling back to a time when he, blissfully, knew nothing. He said it also for his grandparents' house next to a lake in southern Spain, the one where he had spent summers immersed in cold water. For the squalling, disorientating, joyful day in the hospital when his daughter was born. For the youthful summer when he drove across the continent aimlessly, not knowing where he would sleep that night, rejoicing in the freedom of beach and sky and water.

The winter settled in. One panicked day in February, Francis decided to risk finding Clara in the real city. He had never saved her number in his phone, the phone his wife often borrowed, so he had simply memorized it. He had even enjoyed the task at the time, relishing it as proof of his dedication. But he found now that it had gone from his mind completely. He decided instead to cycle past her apartment – just speculatively, he would not speak to her yet, not even really pause, he told himself – but he became lost in the streets of her neighbourhood, the tangle of roads that looked much like any other road, the red-brick buildings and the trees planted alongside, the branches still bare, until he found himself back at his own home, a thin layer of sweat on his body, not even a glimpse of Clara's shadow against lamplight to tide him over.

*

They returned to the city of impermanence not long afterwards. Clara opened her eyes, and noticed that the crack on the ceiling had gone. Clear light streamed through the large window. The bathroom was pristine, the fridge was stocked with their favourite foods. Francis's gamble had taken some time, but it had worked, she realized with joy. The city was once more on their side.

Dailiness

They went to the museum to visit *Still Life with Cherries and Mouse* at once, without discussing it. They walked the whole way. There was such relief in the city restored to them — the colours oversaturated after so long in the real world, the streets clean once more, teeming with other couples, the sound of violins, the restaurants and cafes all open again, even the water of the fountain seeming to flow with extra vigour when they went through the square. It was better than before, even, Clara suggested as they walked, and Francis was happy to agree, dizzy with his gratitude.

That day the painting shimmered with a benevolent energy. It was exactly how they remembered it. The fruits were glossy, the pewter shone, the bread and butter was appetizing, and the candle burned with a steady, fervent light. The mouse was not an intruder but invited in to feast. It was more real than real. It meant everything; it meant nothing.

But it was worth living your life in service of beauty, Clara believed that day. She felt it within her as an undeniable truth. She marvelled at Francis's shoulders in his navy wool jumper. She marvelled that, once more, he appeared to be hers.

Working in the park was good for them. It was a quiet and useful job, satisfying to them both. Rain or sun or neither, it didn't matter, as long as they had their list of tasks, pinned up on the corkboard in the tool shed, and as long as they could complete these tasks with care. One would plant, and one would water. One would prune, the other would weed.

And the days accumulated peacefully. Their arms grew strong with new muscle. They watched, with no small happiness, as the seeds they sowed started to unfurl into green shoots, as the rose bushes they pruned flourished, as the soil grew more fertile. At those times the city of impermanence felt different; soft, grateful to them for their efforts. Perhaps it gained them time, or forgiveness. Clara liked to think so. At the end of their shifts she would snip the most blowsy, browning roses, the ones the caterpillars had got to, and carry them back in her hands, knowing they would be rotten before they even arrived home.

They went to the grocery on their way home one afternoon to buy Clara a chocolate bar, a kind that didn't exist outside of the city, wrapped in pale blue paper with nothing written on it. As he took their coin, Jean paused.

What are you doing now? he asked.

Clara looked at Francis, who shrugged. Nothing, she said.

We're closing for the day in five, Jean said. Would you like to come for a drink?

We'd love to, said Francis, nudging Clara when Jean looked away.

They waited outside while Jean counted the day's takings and Paula switched off the lights, then pulled down the metal grille.

This way, she said, her silver hair pinned roughly on top of her head, a large red bag slung over her arm. She took four bruised apples from it, passing them around. Jean crunched into his loudly.

They walked south, or the direction which Clara had come to think of as south, though it was difficult to fully define compass points within the city. Landmarks and buildings were liable to slide around without warning, fractionally different from day to day; she thought she knew this neighbourhood already, but with Paula leading she quickly lost her bearings. How had they never seen this orchard forested thickly with cherry blossom, its paths strewn with white and pink? They should bring a picnic, she thought, picturing Francis lying, blissful, stretched out upon a blanket.

Have you ever been to the edge of the city? Francis asked them.

You mean the sea? Paula asked. Yes, of course.

Do you know how big it is? asked Francis. Or what's beyond it?

I've no idea, said Paula. I've never seen land on the other side.

I tried to fish there once, Jean said. Paula snorted.

But there's nothing alive in there, he said, shrugging. I had the line in for hours.

Would you have eaten anything you caught? Clara asked. She was hungry.

Jean thought about it. No, he said. On reflection, I would not.

The architecture in Paula and Jean's part of the city was completely different, houses rather than apartments, neat and generously spaced, almost pastoral. Turning into a quieter avenue, Clara saw a cluster of cottages separated from the road by a small thatch of trees. The houses were all painted white and surrounded by flower beds growing riotous plants, fruits, vegetables. Raspberries curled up wooden canes.

Here we are, Jean said, leading them up the path towards a pale yellow door. Excuse the mess.

Inside it was cosy, a little dark, the air cinnamon-scented. Shelves lined the entire room, crammed with books and other objects — ceramic bowls, small metal sculptures, paintings propped up unframed. Clara stood in the middle, overwhelmed.

Kitchen, Paula said, pushing them through to a room at the back, and this one was flooded with light, overlooking another garden. She opened the kitchen door and the air came in. Clara could see that other cottages also backed on to the garden, as if it were a courtyard.

We keep the gardens together, with our neighbours, Paula said with a hint of pride. It's a collaborative effort.

Clara noted the pictures crowding the wall, the fruit trees visible through the doorway.

You've been here a long time, she said.

Yes, said Paula. Jean came up beside her and put his arm around her.

Everyone in this part of the city has, he said. We never go back.

Not at all? asked Francis, shocked.

No, said Jean. We are what are called devotionals. Perhaps you've heard of us.

This is our real world now, said Paula.

Francis glanced with trepidation at Clara.

Jean made them tea, and brought out small, hard almond biscuits from a battered red tin on the counter. Clara sat on a wooden stool, warmed by sunlight. She felt perfectly content. Outside, there were people in the garden – picking strawberries and courgettes, surveying their leaves for holes or rot. Two older men wandered over to the open door.

Felix, Lovro, Paula greeted them. This is Francis and Clara. We wanted to show them the community.

Both men, grey-haired, had the same slightly starved, visceral look about them as Paula and Jean. The city was not necessarily designed for such long stays, Francis thought, taking in the leanness of their arms, the way their veins stood out. But then, what did he know? The heart was adaptable. The rest of the body surely too.

One of the men was carrying a basket of cherries, which he held out to them. Clara took a handful and started to eat them at once. Francis shook his head. They drifted away.

Clara excused herself to go to the bathroom, walking up a flight of white-painted wooden stairs and into a small room containing a large bathtub similar to their own. She washed her hands carefully with the rose-scented soap, ran the pile of the blue hand towel through her fingers. Separated even as they were by a whole floor, she was not feeling the usual ache for Francis, the strange elastic that bound them. She examined the wounds on her body. They were healed now, leaving only smooth discs of pink flesh. Paula and Jean's limbs were scattered with scars, too many to count. They must have left and returned over and over, until they had discovered their trick.

Paula was waiting, shadowy, on the landing. Clara jumped to see her. Before she could say anything, Paula reached out and gripped her arm.

I could tell as soon as I saw you, she said, hushed and reverential.

Clara froze.

I knew it. I knew. I told Jean too.

She was still whispering, her gaze insistent.

Clara glanced behind Paula to the stairs, hoping Francis might come to see what was keeping her. I don't know what you mean, she said, trying to keep her voice steady.

Something in Paula's expression shifted, and suddenly she looked almost maternal.

Oh dear no, you've got me all wrong. Don't panic. You're a student of devotion, like us, she reassured her. I know that's what you are.

Clara blinked. Was it written so clearly on her? Was her need really that bottomless, the real world so easy to renounce? She couldn't even deny it.

Don't be ashamed, said Paula, shaking her arm gently. It's beautiful.

They sat together at the top of the stairs. Paula held Clara's hand with both of hers.

How did you manage to stop leaving? Clara asked.

It took a long time, said Paula. But it can be learned.

She paused.

Belief is a collaborative project, but you can tend to it, create the conditions for it to flourish, she continued. You can nurture it. You can always be more forgiving.

Clara was quiet.

You mean put up with things.

Paula considered this. In a way, she said finally. It's more about self-control. When given the option of hurting someone — so tempting sometimes, I know — how do you step back from it?

But it doesn't stop him hurting me, said Clara. If he wants to leave, I can't stop him.

You can make it so beautiful that he won't want to, said Paula.

Clara was silent. She pulled her hands from Paula's and examined her nails.

You've lost things, am I right? continued Paula, encouragingly. Given up things in the service of this love.

We all have, said Clara.

Paula nodded. Don't let those sacrifices have been in vain. We all begin as tourists. You don't have to carry on that way.

What about the real world? Clara asked.

Paula seemed affronted.

What about it? Wouldn't you rather live in a world designed for you?

Clara thought, for a moment, about what it would mean to leave the real city behind. No more damp apartment, no more gallery. Fine. But no Arturo either. No walking alone along another city's streets on a bright summer morning, unaccountable. No more forests, or train journeys, or cool blue seas. No possibility of a family of her own, no elusive future that could still hypothetically spiral out in any direction, even if she was getting older, even if she appeared to be always standing in place.

Has it been what you wanted? What you've dreamed of? she asked eventually.

Paula smiled, a slow and dreamy smile. Yes, she said. More so than you can imagine.

She stood up. Come and see me next week, she said. Monday night. We'll show you how it's done.

They returned to the kitchen. Francis was leaning against the counter, talking to Jean in a low voice. The late sun hitting his curls, his solemn face animated. He turned at once to her when she entered, like a flower following the light.

Clara woke up to the burning of her forehead with a certain amazement. Francis looked at her in alarm as she lay in the bed, flushed.

I'll take care of you, he said, gallant and unsure.

I feel sick, she said. Oh, I don't want to be sick in front of you.

Francis rummaged in the kitchen cabinets for a mixing bowl and held it to her face the way he had always done for his daughter. Clara retched into it once, twice, and then fell back on to the pillows. He placed it on the floor and smoothed her wet hair back from her brow.

The cherries, Clara said. She sat up to retch again.

Long, feverish sleep. She opened her eyes occasionally to see Francis sitting on a chair in the corner of the room, with the novel they had read so many times before open on his lap.

Where's Arturo? she asked at one point.

At your house, he said, fighting a pang of jealousy. You only have me.

He sat her up and lifted a glass of water to her lips. With her eyes closed she drank at once, abundantly, trusting.

It was three days before she was returned to full health, three days of Francis caring for her. He did not become frustrated by her demands, or her helplessness, the way they both secretly feared he might. Docile and sleepy, she was easy to care for. Easier, perhaps, to love that way.

She came to enjoy feeling dependent on him, weak in their shared bed, waiting for his cool hand at her brow. She accepted soup spooned into her mouth, dry toast, ginger ale.

On the second day she was more irritable, snapping at him when he tried to change the sweat-soaked T-shirt she was sleeping in. This was the only note of discord, and he enacted a tiny revenge – nothing so serious as harm, he felt – by failing to go to her immediately, later on, when she was back in the bed and calling for water.

I didn't hear you, my love, he told her, bringing her a glass brimming with ice in compensation. He had only hesitated for five minutes, listening to the sound of her disconsolate voice with guilt, and some pleasure. She needed him. He found, uneasily, that it gave him a sense of security, a sense of power. He pressed his lips to the damp crown of her head.

I didn't hear you at all.

Over time, in the real city, Clara had developed a system of rituals and bargains for the days before she saw Francis. There were foods she could not eat – seafood, raw vegetables, food cooked elsewhere than her kitchen – because she was struck by the fear that she might get food poisoning and be unable to see him. There were things she could not do – drive fast, most sports, travel – in case she might injure herself. She could not even leave the city, in case she was delayed in her return or suffered an accident on the way. These superstitions had an element of both safe-keeping, and of denial. If she lived ascetically, at least temporarily, she would somehow earn the joy of seeing him, or repent in advance for the seeing of him. For living a life that was outside of her life, for borrowing a person who wasn't hers.

These things she could control, but she couldn't control what was happening to him. She couldn't do anything about a sick child, a suspicious wife, an emergency department meeting, a deadline, a change of heart. She worried that his car might crash, that he might fall ill, that he might grow bored of her, that he might vanish entirely. She could not relax even on the days when they saw each other until she heard his knock on the door. She lived perhaps even more for those seconds when she walked to answer it than for the time they spent together; the unbearable, syrupy moments between desire's anticipation and its satisfaction, when all else fell away.

Now, living as Clara did, permanently in desire's satisfaction, she occasionally missed those moments. But there were new things. She felt devotional towards the maintenance of their life in the city, valuing even the smallest and most banal details. If the kitchen counters needed wiping, it was because they had cooked something, taken it into their bodies. If the sheets needed changing, it was because those same bodies had slept and fucked on top of them. If the surfaces needed dusting, it was because time enough had passed to accumulate dust, and an accumulation of time also meant an accumulation of love. She delighted even in the light film of dirt on the bathroom windowsill, a bloom threatening mould from the shower's condensation, running her finger along it. The ordinariness was more transgressive than any hotel, more private than any secret, more thrilling than any stolen hour.

On the Monday, they made their way back to Paula and Jean's house. They had only gone a street or two from their apartment when Clara stopped. There was a gap in a row of tall, old-fashioned apartment buildings – a clean break right in the middle, the buildings either side totally untouched. Residents sat out on their small balconies as usual; life continued in the buildings still existing. All that was left of the disappeared one was a neat square of what appeared to be blue plastic tarpaulin, covering the ground. As they stared, it seemed to ripple. Clara stepped forward to get a closer look.

Don't, Francis said, struck by a sudden dread.

Clara paused. She could see a corner of red, silty earth, just where the tarpaulin didn't quite meet the ground. The people on the balconies craned down to see what was happening.

Don't! Don't! they called to her once they realized what she was doing, waving their arms. Clara stepped back, and she and Francis continued, without further discussion.

Paula hugged them both warmly, tightly, as if she were their mother.

I want to show you something, she said, breaking away, addressing Clara. It's only for you.

She shrugged apologetically at Francis. Jean is outside, though, in the shed. Go and see him.

Francis and Clara looked at each other.

It'll only take an hour, Paula said to Francis. Go on outside, now.

Clara followed Paula up the stairs. She could hear voices, diffuse as the sound of bees. When Paula pushed open the door to a room Clara hadn't noticed before, the voices stilled.

Welcome, Clara, Paula said.

The room was entirely white. The floorboards, the walls, the closed curtains, made of a heavy and lustrous material. Six people sat on wooden chairs in a circle. They raised their hands in greeting. She recognized the two grey-haired men from before. There were two empty seats.

Jean would normally join us, Paula said, sitting with some difficulty in one of the free chairs. Please, Clara, take a seat.

They sat in silence for several minutes. Clara waited for something to happen. Then Paula reached over, switched off the lamp in the corner and started to hum: a single note, held unwavering, low and unearthly. There was a pause of a few seconds, and the others joined in, one by one. Clara did not know whether she should copy them, but soon she stopped worrying, as she lapsed into a quiet, insistent calm. Her eyes closed of their own accord. The humming broke off.

Circle of lovers, Paula spoke into its absence, in a ringing voice. Students of devotion. Touch and be touched.

With ritual formality, the circle joined hand to hand. Clara did it easily, as if used to it.

Be present in your devotion, Paula intoned. Be there fully, and be there now.

Clara stepped into her devotion as if it were another place entirely. She did not visit the worlds they had created in the past – the thick hotel carpets as a proxy for grasslands, the sheets as lakes, her apartment as a universe.

Devotion, it turned out, was mostly formless. It was a landscape of glowing white. Landscape was the wrong word, perhaps. It was still, and soft, stretching for ever and nowhere.

From outside the landscape, Clara could hear Paula continuing to talk.

You will not be cruel, she said. You do not contain cruelty. You are in love's service. There is nothing within you but boundless joy.

Clara breathed. The white light around her pulsed. She was overcome by a sense of bliss.

Think of the one you love, Paula said. Forgive the one you love. For we are here, now, and we are together, and all will be as it should.

Francis was sitting outside in the garden with Jean, the lawn lit up with tiny solar lamps. They were drinking home-made wine. Francis leapt up as the others filed past him to their own homes. Paula presented Clara to him with pride.

Here she is, she said. She did well.

Clara left Paula's side, and put her arms around Francis tightly. He lifted his hand to her hair, disconcerted by the strength of her embrace. She pressed her face to the wool of his jumper and cried for a moment. He misread it as laughter.

Hello, he said. I'm glad to see you too.

On the way home she tried to explain what had happened. Francis seemed frustrated.

Did they drug you? he pressed. Did you see visions?

No, she said. Not exactly.

She felt unsteady, hollowed out and euphoric both.

You're pale, Francis said, once they had got into the apartment and switched the lights on. Let me run you a bath.

He was solicitous, loving. Clara sat, limp, in the hot water. He knelt next to the tub, poured lavender oil under the taps. The pipes creaked. She put out a wet hand to his face and turned it to hers. His eyes were concerned. They met hers easily. He pushed her dark hair, damp with sweat, behind her ears.

Do you want to stay? she asked. To stay for always.

Francis turned off the taps. He didn't answer but leaned forward and kissed her deeply. The sting of his stubble, the slight heat rising from under his shirt collar, brought her back into the room, into the apartment, into the world they had built together.

Home, she thought with longing, watching him as he put his hand under the water to check the temperature. She remembered Arturo, washing her hair. How he had warned her.

But there was no bad or good in the city of impermanence. There was only harm or harm's absence. The world, that slow and breathing animal. Alive to the fluctuations they lived within.

She slept heavily. Woke to calm sky. Francis already awake, watching her. Quiet, distinct from silence. Quiet, thick and soft, insulating the city.

Will you come upstairs with me next time? she asked him.

I'll try it, he said. If it's that important to you.

On their way to work, they walked past a jewellery shop that they had never seen before. They stopped to admire the window full of shining rings.

Let's go in, Francis said, feeling reckless.

They were guided to a small, neat desk in the centre of the

shop, encouraged to sit and accept an espresso each, as trays of rings were brought out for them to admire.

Which ones do you like? Francis asked, running his finger along the black velvet casing.

Clara chose one of white gold with a small opal set into it. She held out both her hands to him. When Francis pushed the band on to her ring finger, it seemed to her that she might die of happiness. He let out a long exhale.

That felt good, he said.

Clara admired it on her hand.

He caught the jeweller's eye. We'll take it, he said. He handed over the contents of his wallet.

They walked out into the weak sunlight. Clara fiddled with the ring on her finger, where it was already stuck, as if glued into place.

An envelope under the door. An invitation from Lili and Adan, green ink on thick paper, a restaurant they didn't know. Their names, written together.

I don't really like them, you know, Francis said later, as they dressed for dinner.

Why not? asked Clara.

They're a little brash. Not my kind of people.

Who are your kind of people? she asked, brushing her hair.

Quieter people, he said.

Should we try and join an adulterers' book club? she suggested. Maybe there's a chess society?

Forget it, said Francis, laughing.

Lili's a loose cannon, said Clara. I wish I knew their deal.

Ask them, said Francis.

I will. See, we'll have lots to talk about, said Clara, putting the hairbrush down.

More things arrived in the apartment from time to time, wished for or willed or simply needed. In the reflection of a mirror that had appeared overnight on the wall, white-painted metal and ornate, Clara put on a pair of blue glass earrings she had found in the pocket of a dress in the wardrobe. She blotted her red lips. Francis appeared behind her in the mirror, kissed her shoulder, the nape of her neck. Then he was gone.

*

Lili and Adan were already there when they arrived, a bottle of pink champagne in a misted silver bucket next to the table. Clara kissed the other couple in greeting.

So good to see you both, she said. She felt enlivened by their presence. It was like she had known them for years.

Lili shrieked. Is that a gorgeous new ring? she asked, snatching up Clara's hand to examine it closer, then dropping it. I love it.

The pink champagne went down easily. Adan was next to Clara, wearing a livid purple tie that she hated.

Amazing colour, she said, pointing at it.

Thanks, said Adan, glancing at Lili. I wasn't sure.

Oh no – it's perfect, said Clara.

The starters arrived, though nobody had ordered. Steak tartare topped with glistening raw egg yolks, scallops seared in butter, crayfish salad and a truffled potato soup. Clara took the tartare. She punctured the yolk with the tip of her knife.

Tell me, how did you both get together? she asked Adan, who brightened.

We met through work, actually, said Adan. I was assigned to a new project, in another city, and the moment I walked into the office I saw her. Or heard her, rather.

He laughed, looking across at Lili.

Do you know how loud she is when she shouts? he continued. When she really gets going?

I was having a bad day! Lili protested from across the table, shrugging extravagantly.

Anyway, I was scared of her at first, he said, turning his attention back to Clara. But the team went out that night and we all got pretty drunk. All I could think about was losing the others and being alone with her. It turned out she was thinking the same.

And that was ten years ago? asked Clara.

Yes, said Adan, meditatively. Ten whole years.

Wow, said Clara.

Adan nodded. What do you do? he asked. In the *other place*, I mean.

I work at a gallery, said Clara.

Both creative types, Adan said, in a tone that was hard to read.

Francis is, said Clara. But I don't do much, to be honest.

She's an artist, interjected Francis from across the table. When she wants to be.

I'm really not, said Clara.

Another bottle of pink champagne arrived and was summarily dispensed into the glasses. She finished the tartare in silence.

Have you ever been married? Adan asked Clara.

No, said Clara.

Would you like to be? asked Adan.

Loving him sort of gets in the way, said Clara, gesturing briefly at Francis.

It doesn't rule it out, he said.

I guess I'm very conventional, then, she said.

Adan nodded. Well, you've got less to lose. If that's any consolation.

Clara thought about the possibilities of her future, narrowing into a waiting room.

Yes. It's much simpler, she said.

Adan gestured across the table for the others to raise their glasses, as he proposed a toast.

To love, he said. To true love.

Clara looked towards Francis, who was smiling but didn't quite meet her eyes, staring at a point just beyond her head.

*

Clara stood up to go to the bathroom. It was so dark in the corridor that she almost missed the framed print of *Still Life with Cherries and Mouse* that hung, unobtrusive, by the door. Even like this — reproduced, flattened, hardly visible in the tasteful darkness — it was beautiful, moving, in ways she could not explain, in ways that made her feel unsettled.

In the bathroom she washed her hands, checked her lipstick. She remembered the disarticulated feeling she had had on her first day in the city, staring down at her hands in a bathroom just like this, love songs playing on the speakers, the towels thick and clean. She sat for a moment on the pink-upholstered chair in the corner of the room, dizzy.

When she returned to the table, Francis was explaining to the others how they had met. Her glass was full again; she drank half down immediately, still standing, and felt calmer. Steaks were on everybody's plates, pooling in their blood. Francis met her eyes. She realized he was drunker than she had ever seen him.

I saw her in front of a painting, he said.

She had never heard him tell this story before. She sat down to listen.

It was agreed they should all go on somewhere, once the brandy was finished and the petits fours too, which Lili had pushed away and which Clara, always voracious, had eaten right off her plate along with her own.

It was dark as they spilled out of the restaurant, the city gold-lit, warm, bustling with life. Three perfect stars hung in the sky beside a pink moon. Francis stumbled on the cobbles, and Clara took his elbow. Lili and Adan went up ahead, staggering, with their arms around each other.

Whoops, Francis said, righting himself. He started laughing.

You got our first meeting wrong, Clara said.

No, I didn't, he said. I remember it perfectly.

You made it sound like I chased you, she said.

Yes. Single-minded in your pursuit, he said. Ruthless when you want something. Isn't that you?

He twirled her around. Her body was stiff, reluctant.

Do we have to go to the nightclub? he asked, letting her go and falling back into uncoordinated step. They're two of the dullest people I've ever met.

Have you always been this judgemental? she wondered aloud.

I just want to be with you, he said. Everyone else here is a nightmare.

We're not better than them, she said.

Yes, we are, he said. They met at *work*.

Life can't just contain two people, she said.

Why can't it? he asked. He put a loose arm around her neck. His breath was sour.

A shared life has friends in it, she said. She didn't say the word *witnesses*, though she thought it.

Friends, he said, as if the idea had never occurred to him before.

Would your friends like me? she asked, unable to stop herself.

Well, it would be complicated by the whole cheating-on-Iona thing, he said.

Clara felt ice in her stomach. She didn't want a name. He withdrew his arm.

Whoops, he said again, idiotically. For a moment Clara hated him – truly hated him. She wondered if he had done it on purpose.

It's fine, she said. He looked sideways at her.

Actually, no, it's not fine, she said.

It was an accident, he said, his voice louder now. I'm with you, aren't I? I'm right here with you.

Temporarily, she said. It's only ever temporary.

When did you get so petty? he asked. So sensitive.

Clara paced on, looking straight ahead. He waved his hands, dismissively.

I thought you were above those little jealous stereotypes.

Well, I suppose I'm not.

Lili and Adan were far ahead now. They turned around.

Stop whispering sweet nothings and get over here! they shouted. While the night is still young!

Adan swept Lili up over his shoulder in a fireman's lift, and she screamed.

The night, the night! Francis thought bitterly. That long and empty expanse which could hold so many terrors, so many possibilities, and which now, here, held the capability to tear him and Clara asunder. Yes, he supposed they should make the most of the nights, the magical and incomprehensible and impossible nights!

He watched Clara run towards Adan and Lili. She didn't look behind her, didn't check that he would follow. For a long time, half-witnessed and only occasionally in his life, she had felt like someone he dreamed into being, a creature playing at a life in sweet, darting stabs, like a baby animal tentatively creating a shelter. And then one day there she was, expansive and whole and formed, a person with a life beyond him, a person he did not understand. There were times back in the real world when he had taken his eyes off her, weeks at a time, and her life went on without him – her life which was her real life, as much as she liked to tell him the opposite, that she lived entirely in those hotel days, the world that only he witnessed.

In that unwatched time she had blossomed, or hardened. It had startled him to realize this.

He was tempted just to leave, to abandon the whole sorry evening where it stood. But then he remembered, of course, that he couldn't do that. He was stuck to her, stuck with her. Already the elastic that bound them was complaining. So he walked towards the three of them; they were laughing, Lili somehow on the ground now, the black maw of the metro station waiting to take them onwards.

They took the train to the edge of the city, swinging from the yellow plastic straps. The journey sobered Francis, somewhat. The nightclub was large, a building that had once been some sort of warehouse. They approached two imposing men, dressed in black, who nodded and let them pass. The bass trembled through Francis's feet.

In the daytime the windows of the top floor would overlook the red earth and the water beyond it, but for now all they could see were their own reflections. The four of them stood together holding bottles of beer, peering out into the dark. The beers were so cold. Clara felt that she could drink a thousand of them. She *could* drink a thousand of them. There was nothing she could not do. The city pulsed through her. *Thank you*, she told it. Thank you.

She took another sip and turned to see Francis still staring out of the window, and was struck by the desire to walk downstairs and out of the club and towards the unseen ring of water, to feel the red earth under her feet and the shock of the water's cold as she stepped into it and let it cover her.

Lili pulled Francis along through the crowd, the four of them downstairs now, where the music was louder, much louder, brutal and intricate. Her elegant dress was out of place and patched with sweat, clinging, but she wore it well. Lili would survive anywhere, Francis thought, watching how easily she moved through the crowd. Clara would too.

They stopped in a small pocket of space. Open your mouths, said Adan, and when they did, obediently, he placed a pill on to each of their tongues one by one. Clara and Lili swallowed at once, washing it down with their beers. Adan put one in his own mouth, raised his bottle to Francis, who could feel his own pill, pebble-like, in his mouth. Down the hatch, he said, not breaking eye contact, and they both swallowed.

On the dancefloor, Francis's hand caught Clara's wrist where it hung at her side, his other hand at the small of her back, pulling her close to him. Her lips were hard and soft at once. Her mouth opened, and then she moved her body against his.

Dance, she commanded him, stepping back, a new self-possession. Skin pearlescent, flawless, in the low light. The music felt overpowering. He wanted to sink into it, but he felt afraid of doing so, of losing himself entirely. Adan and Lili danced with abandon, their eyes closed.

Bathroom! he shouted into Clara's ear, and she nodded, turning to the others and falling in sync with them, her arms raised above her head. It took a while to push his way off the dancefloor, strangers' bodies pressing and surging like a wave, and he felt panic blooming in his stomach, then the relief of stepping into the cool of the corridor. It was long and winding, so dark it was difficult to see anything, full of couples entwined or leaning against the walls in intense conversation. He felt the invisible elastic that attached him to Clara starting to stretch.

The queue for the bathroom was long. As he waited, he

noticed a woman, alone and crying, leaning against the other side of the corridor. She looked familiar, and he realized it was the waitress who had told him to get a job.

Hey, he said, raising his hand. She looked up at him, tear-stained, in faint blue light. He crossed over to her side of the corridor, rested his cheek against the damp wall next to her. Slouch of his shoulder, the distant sound of electronica.

You'll lose your place, she said, turning to him.

Their faces were close. He put his hand to her neck, without really registering what he was doing. Her other must have been close. His whole body was a throb of light. He felt an incapacitating softness for every person on the earth, but especially for the waitress, at this moment, her sharp features and the dark make-up smudged below her eyes. She paused for a moment, then offered up her mouth to him.

Clara felt a stunning pain at her temples. She put her hand to her head and crouched down. Her eyes watered. It hurts, it hurts, she said, when Lili took hold of her shoulders and shook her and asked what was wrong.

Francis went into the bathroom, alone. He was shaking. He washed his hands in the sink, over and over, and tried to remove his wedding ring again. It did not move. In the mirror he checked his wild eyes, his pale face. The elastic had wrapped around his chest, a band of enormous pressure, so that for one terrible moment he couldn't breathe at all. Then a pain in his wrist. Looking down to his hands, he saw blood coursing down to join the water in the sink. *No*, he thought – *no, no, no*. The wound was larger than the others had been, ragged at the edges. He waited for the bleeding to slow, pulled the sleeve of his shirt down to cover it, but not before a man washing his hands in the sink next to him had noticed. He looked at Francis with sympathy. Sorry, my friend, he said.

By the time he reached Clara on the dancefloor, the pain in her head had passed, the pill lifting her back up.

I want to go home, said Francis.

But the music is just getting good, said Clara. Don't you want to stay for a bit longer?

No, he said. I want to go home.

They were far from home, but neither of them wanted to get the metro. The night air was pellucid, thick with residual heat. Darkness everywhere. The warehouse district seemed to go on for a long time, longer than Francis would have imagined – the red scrubbed earth visible under cracked pavement, the occasional anaemic weed growing out of it.

Towards the centre the streets were deserted and very calm, and the pale, old-fashioned buildings all had their windows shuttered. Some of them were falling into disrepair. It was strange to see the restaurants and cafes of their favourite square silent, empty, the chairs stacked away. They sat on the edge of the fountain and trailed their hands in the water as the sky smoothly brightened above them, as if by dimmer switch.

It was light by the time they arrived at their apartment. Clara kicked off her shoes at the mat and went straight to the bathroom. She brushed her teeth vigorously. Her eyes were large and dark in the mirror. She passed out before Francis could reach the bed, naked, the covers thrown off her body.

Francis showered, briefly, watching the blood running down the plughole as if it were very little to do with him. Wrapped in a towel, he watched her from the doorway for a while. Those dirty soles, her tousled hair. Her skin seemed to radiate heat even from where he stood.

Perhaps she was not who he thought she was. The person he had believed her to be. She was resilient, perceptive. She laughed easily and did not hold grudges, least of all against him. He knew these things, or thought he did. How could he ever be sure? Her potential for unknowability felt overwhelming. In his mind he saw a hundred, a thousand, versions of Clara reflected, each one impossible to fully predict.

Francis remembered the summer rain of the day they had first met; how it had made his shirt cling to his neck, a not unpleasant sensation. He was supposed to be at work, but the weather had changed as he was walking back to the university after a meeting elsewhere, and he had ducked into the museum just for a few minutes. There was nothing urgent, and he would not be missed if he were to luxuriate in beauty for a moment or two.

He remembered how it had felt to see Clara for the first time, standing in front of *Still Life with Cherries and Mouse*. Her hair wet and hanging down her back, the rain dampening her pretty, faded dress. The whole picture pleasing but strange, imperfect, until she had turned partly, and he saw her in profile, light and shadow, the clean lines of her nose and mouth, and he knew he had to touch her. She had turned fully then, to face him – perhaps sensing he was looking – and he had met her gaze for a while before walking into the next room, wondering what she would do.

And she had followed. And when they were both circling in that room, she walked ahead of him, as if asking a question. Would he follow? And he followed, of course. He went slowly. The low heels of her sandals clicked. The museum was so quiet, apart from the sound of the rain on the roof.

He could have moved with her all day. He loved the

attentiveness of her body; how she paused in front of the paintings, head held high, waiting for his next cue. How she stared, fixedly, at whatever was in front of her, absorbed in it in order to pretend she was not absorbed in him. He reached out his hand to her, hovering over her vertebrae, then dropped it. He wanted to delay the moment when he would touch her, to stretch it out until it vibrated, glowing, in the air between them.

There was no going back there, he knew now, to the people they were. And there was no going back from it. A whole other life had been set in motion. The possibilities for what love could feel like, for what love could do, gathered around them.

That was how they knew each other best, most truly: as two bodies, loosened from the real world's bearings, in a light-filled room.

In the restaurant with Lili and Adan he had watched her greet them both with ease, watched her compliment Adan's ugly tie, watched her appear genuinely interested in the story of how they had met. He was jealous, he had realized, just before the starters arrived. She was the way with others that she was with him, even with people he did not like.

And then their painting on the wall by the bathroom. The city was sly and unrelenting – the city would not leave him alone. He had tried to ignore the print, but he couldn't. He had felt the sudden, irrational urge to find a steak knife and rip the canvas. This reproduction was garish, flat, the paper visibly cheap. It made ugly what should be beautiful, made visible what should remain unseen.

When he arrived back at the table, he set to drinking in earnest. Everything was nightmarish: the ostentatious food they could no longer afford, Lili with her nails and her perfume leaning into him as if they were old confidants, the spinning lights, even the waiters balletic in their pairs.

Lili was addressing him, animated. Francis tried to gather himself to listen.

I feel like we've barely spoken, she was saying. It was clear to Francis that she already didn't like him. But that was fine. He took another long drink.

We haven't, he said.

Well, let's rectify that, said Lili. I'm really fond of Clara, you know. I'm so glad you're both here.

Me too, said Francis. She's incredible.

She's frivolous, he thought. *She's insincere. She has poor judgement in people. She wants everyone to love her.* He took another sip of his champagne, feeling vindictive.

How did you meet again? Lili asked.

There was a painting, he said. I saw her in front of a painting.

He looked across the table to Clara, who had just sat down. The curve of her neck. The softness of her gaze. Still, he loved her. He almost could not speak with how much he loved her. But they were waiting for him to share the story of how they had met, the story of her wet-haired, looking at a painting she didn't know anything about. He opened his mouth to tell it.

Return

When Clara woke up in the real city, the shock almost undid her. She opened her eyes, then closed them again. No, no, no, she whispered.

She was filled with an unadulterated, seething rage at Francis: at this person who gave her everything, and then had the power to simply take it away.

Francis woke up and then fell back asleep for a long time before waking properly, bleary, barely distinguishing world from world. He phoned in sick to the university.

Poor Francisco, Iona said, when he finally came downstairs.

It was rare that she ever used his full name. Possibly it had been years. Private language, unpractised.

He kissed the top of her head with no small amount of guilt. He ached, suddenly, for a version of them that had dissipated without him noticing, for his part in this dissipation. A rush of heat, and of grief, then gone. Could a body really be this fickle? he wondered, in disgust. How many loves, or echoes of love, could someone hold?

One day, two, three. Clara lapsed from rage back into grief, from vengefulness back into paralysis. She noticed new grey hairs at her temple and spent some time examining them. Time continued to enact itself on her body. Perhaps it was another cost of movement between the worlds. In the real world, unlike the unreal, the seasons were changing. The leaves were starting to bud and burst forth. They no longer woke up to frost.

It was like breathing water, Francis felt, as he held his daughter's hand, walking her to school. He had become acclimatized to the wrong things. Now he missed even the cramping feeling of the elastic that bound him to Clara.

His daughter was sullen, lagging behind him. When they passed an empty can she kicked it like a football, shimmying it down the pavement, then kicking it again. Stop that, Francis told her nicely. She looked at him and then, with what seemed like genuine malice, kicked it again. It skittered into the road. He tugged her forward, taken aback.

His absences were creating an atmospheric disturbance even without being visible in the real world – it seemed obvious to him. How long could he keep getting away with it?

Clara went reluctantly with Arturo to a party, sitting on a sofa in the corner all evening and watching the others dance, talk, flirt. She felt translucent, speechless. He pulled her, finally, to the bathroom. Outside they heard music, a spray of laughter. She had never seen him so angry.

It's a waste, Clara, he said. It's a fucking waste to live like this.

Clara turned wordlessly and stormed out, down the hallway and down the stairs and all the way out into the cold street, her breath streaming vapour, and then she ran as far as she could manage, collapsing on to a seat at a bus stop when she could go no further. Running a marathon? commented the only other person at the bus stop, a tiny old woman wrapped in layers of ragged black and wearing an oversized straw hat. Clara didn't answer. The air of the night was cold and sordid, all was malevolent, and she turned up the collar of her jacket and shrank into it as she waited, waited, waited.

At a children's birthday party in their local park, Francis stood with the other fathers near a table set with sandwiches and sugared biscuits and drank the beer handed to him, dutiful, not tasting it. He observed the other fathers as if they were a different species: some attentive, others glued to their phone, some implausibly young in artful trainers and others so weary he would have assumed them to be grandfathers. Did they ever wake up in another city, next to a familiar and unfamiliar body? There was talk of mortgages, of the opening of a new activity centre. The nearby children screamed in a delight that the adults could no longer fathom. He could see Elise at the outskirts with two small girls, clutching half a cupcake and wearing a look of stocky determination. His heart felt as if it must surely give way. One father in a crumpled blue jacket held a small baby asleep in a carrier on his chest. Francis smiled at him and the father smiled back, tired, proud. Francis didn't feel himself one of them. But he hadn't belonged at Adan and Lili's narcissists' convention, either.

Clara went to the launch of an exhibition. The artist was a friend of a friend, younger than her, made paintings with gouache so thick you could stand a spoon in it. She watched them basking in their success across the room as she quickly drank a glass of warm white wine, made small talk with distant friends who exclaimed to see her.

Where have you been? asked a girl in a long leather coat.

I've always been around, Clara said, defensive. I don't go anywhere.

Another acquaintance turned out to be pregnant. Clara couldn't stop herself staring at her stomach, the sheer obviousness of it. The acquaintance didn't seem to notice, or was gracious about it.

What should I do? Clara asked herself, later that night, as she sat on the tiny, illegal roof terrace that she shared with the others in the building, her knees bunched up against her chest. The stars barely visible, the horizon weighed down with orange smog, as she waited.

You must cleave the desire from the object, came the answer from her conscience. *You must understand it as hunger within yourself, and not an embodied urge.*

But it is in his body, in him, that the desire was born, Clara argued.

A body is a body, it argued back. *It's your desire that's singular. It's the lack that gives birth to the desire.*

I did not understand desire before him. I barely thought of desire before him.

You would forget him sooner than you think if you lost him.

He and only he is the desire, Clara insisted, shaken by how her own belief could fail her.

Francis slept a lot, collapsing into bed by ten each night, not waking or even moving until the next morning. He dreamed of starry skies, of a fissure cleaving the ground so deeply that there was no end to be found.

Clara woke into total stillness one morning and thought, still half-asleep, that there was a clarity in being alone, there was a peace. A few moments before yearning kicked back in. The narrative of her love wavered, flared back up like a candle's flame. Re-established itself in the service of adoration.

I would do anything to return, she thought.
   I would do anything to return, he thought.

Three weeks sleeping at different ends of the same city. And on the twenty-second day, in the city of impermanence, they awoke to the wail of a child.

The Family

Sharp light. The sound of a high-pitched siren that was not a siren. Clara felt herself sunk in a deeper sleep than usual, struggling to wake. She sat up with difficulty, her body heavy. At the end of the bed was a wicker bassinet. Francis was already awake, standing, looking at whatever was contained within.

What's going on? Clara asked.

Francis did not answer. Clara pulled herself out of bed and went to the bassinet. Inside was a newborn baby, red and balled up. It screamed and screamed.

There's been some kind of mistake, Francis said.

Clara acted involuntarily. She reached into the bassinet and lifted the baby up to her. She and Francis had woken up naked, the way they always did. Pins and needles in her nipples, the nerves singing. Immediately the baby started nudging at her breast, and she moved to the sofa as Francis watched in astonishment. The baby latched on, started to feed. She had never done this before, but it felt somehow easy. There was milk; the baby drank. She looked down at the crumpled face, the shock of dark damp hair.

There, there, sweetheart, Clara murmured.

When she looked up at Francis, she saw only horror in his face.

*

Clara had not been around that many babies. She did not feel particularly strongly about them either way. But this one – she loved him, somehow. She knew she loved him. She felt her way through the love, towards the love, as if it were a fine, misted rain.

The baby was a boy. He looked how Francis's daughter had looked when she was born. Clara did not know this, but Francis did. He watched Clara nurse the mysterious infant, who quietened quickly. It seemed too strange, the three of them naked, as though spat into some primal scene. He dressed quickly, feeling a kind of shame.

I'll go and find someone to tell, he said, faltering. Someone to sort this out.

The baby was drowsy now, eyes flickering shut. Clara stroked his soft cheek with her finger.

Hold him, she said, turning to Francis and serving up the child. He recoiled from the sight of the milk still beading her skin.

Put him down, Clara, he ordered. Get dressed.

Clara looked at him for a long time before she put the baby down carefully in the bassinet, then walked to the wardrobe, pulled a yellow cotton dress carelessly over her body. The milk spotted through at once.

Don't you want to wash? Francis asked her, cringing a little at the harshness of his voice.

Clara didn't answer. She returned to the bassinet and took up the baby once more.

Put him down, Francis said again.

No, she said.

There was a pram by the door of the apartment now. When Clara pulled open the chest of drawers next to the wardrobe she found white cotton one-pieces, tiny, brand new. She took the baby to the bathroom and closed and locked the door behind them. There was a small plastic tub nestled into the main bathtub, and a neat stack of disposable nappies under the sink next to the bandages and antiseptic. She closed the lid of the toilet and sat down, cradling the still-naked baby. He was sleeping. She had the sense that she was witnessing something that should not be witnessed, mesmerized by his cheeks, his hands, the little nails.

She did shower, in the end, leaving the baby in a nest of towels on the floor, keeping her eyes on him the whole time. Out of the shower, she hesitated for a while before kneeling on the floor and putting a nappy on him. She had never done it before. He was awake again now, but quiet, moving his legs in the air as she peeled off the tabs and fastened the padding around him. She returned to Francis with hair wet, the yellow dress back on, the baby in her arms. He was on the sofa, staring straight ahead.

I think we should go for a walk, Clara said. The three of us.

Clara carried the baby down the stairs, Francis handling the pram with practised ease. When they reached the lobby she tucked the baby into the pram, arranging the blankets around him in a way that seemed right, but he started to cry at once. Francis watched, then pushed her gently aside.

He's too warm, he said. Like this, look.

The baby quietened and Francis manoeuvred the pram out of the door, then relinquished it to Clara. Outside it was incredibly bright. There was nobody else around.

The city was empty. Nobody in the square, nobody in the cafes, though the chairs and tables were all laid out. Francis went into their usual cafe while Clara waited outside with the pram.

Hello? he called, walking all the way back into the kitchen. There was nobody there, but the lights were on. Chopping boards of yellow and red plastic were laid on the wooden counters with knives set neatly alongside, and the fridge, when he opened it, was full of salads and sandwiches. He took a tuna sandwich and a ham-and-cheese sandwich, guiltily, bringing them back outside.

They sat at one of the tables to eat. They were both starving. Clara moved the pram with one hand and held her sandwich with the other. The baby woke up before she could finish it, fussing and mewling. She left the crust on the table and lifted him into her arms at once.

You don't have to pick him up straight away when he cries, Francis said.

But he's hungry, she said.

She was right. The baby nestled into her skin. Francis tried to will up some tenderness, but it was too uncanny. The infant's blue eyes, their resemblance to his daughter's, the baby in Clara's arms, she who he had never thought about in those terms. It was like an untuned note on a piano.

Take him, Clara urged Francis again once the baby had been fed.

I don't want to, Francis said baldly.

Don't you want to know how it feels to hold him? Just for a moment? Clara persisted.

He's not real. It doesn't bear thinking about, he said.

He's real, she said.

You didn't want him, he said. You insisted. We agreed.

Clara didn't react. The damage was done.

Pre-emptive grief. She was felled by love, even knowing that they did not have much time, even knowing as she did that the creature she held in her arms could not exist. And yet – he was warm. He had a surprising solidity. Remember this, she told herself, the way she had told herself so many times before.

The deserted city felt eerie at first, but quickly she was grateful for it. She didn't want anyone to witness Francis's cruelty towards the child, his disavowal, his refusal to touch him unless necessary. More than that, she did not want anyone to intrude on this time with her baby. She didn't even want Francis there, she realized. She would rather be alone with the child. Alone with the child and the city.

There had been no question of keeping the pregnancy. They had spoken of it in pragmatic terms. Francis had seemed relieved by how brisk she was able to be about it.

Path not taken. Path that was never a path.

In the park, they found shade under a tree. Empty boats bobbed on the lake, blue and white. Clara lay on the ground and laid the baby on her chest, froglike, splayed. She was hungry again. Francis went to the nearby ice-cream stand, seemingly abandoned, and rifled through its contents, returning with an industrial-sized tub of strawberry gelato, two flimsy plastic spoons. They ate in silence.

Clara watched him walking to the bins with their empty tub and spoons, walking back. Are you hurt? she asked. You're walking strangely.

There was a pain in his foot, Francis realized. He slipped off his shoe and saw at once the bloom of red through his sock. The fabric clung, bloody, to his skin. Clara watched as he peeled it off.

Well, there we go, she said.

*

She changed the baby again, growing in confidence. She blew a raspberry on his stomach. Francis lay on the grass, so still, she thought he might have fallen asleep. Her eyes were wet, and they stung in the unrelenting sunlight. She wanted him to feel pleased about the baby, for this day they had with him, knowing it would be the only one.

This is not fair, she told the city silently. Why would you show me this? After all I've done for you.

They pushed the pram down the middle of the main road, no cars in sight. The traffic lights flashed pointlessly. The baby had started to cry again in the park, but when the pram was moving he slept, and so they remained in perpetual motion.

They stopped at an empty restaurant to feed him again. Clara held the baby to her skin, watching the sunset come down as usual.

Isn't it beautiful? she asked the baby. He held her smallest finger with his tiny hand, eyes unfocused.

Francis came back from the kitchen with only bread and olives. Wine, which Clara refused to drink. They ate messily, quietly. They left the remains of the meal there.

As they walked back to the apartment, Clara kept the baby in her arms. Francis pushed the empty pram. When they reached their building, she walked ahead of him, swiftly, entering the apartment and settling herself on the sofa. Even that distance was enough to feel the tug of whatever string bound her and Francis, but she ignored it. She was alone with her baby, the only chance they would have, and she wept as she kissed him on his little face.

Thank you, she told him.

When Francis entered the room, she didn't acknowledge him. She remained motionless, with the baby in her arms, as he passed through to the bathroom and then the bedroom, stayed there until long after Francis had fallen asleep. Soft night outside; the light of one table lamp, in the corner. She stared at the baby until her eyes blurred with tiredness, and then took him to the bedroom, placed him gently in the bassinet. He cooed like a bird. She watched him settle. As soon as she lay down, exhaustion took over. She was gone in seconds.

Return

Clara woke into the real world with no surprise.

Francis went immediately to the bedroom of his daughter, still asleep, and watched her from the doorway. She had been an easy child. It had been an easy life. He wondered what life with Clara and their child would have been like. He was not able to wonder it dispassionately.

In the dark kitchen, everyone else still asleep, he cried bent over the counter. He cried for the way the baby's hand had swung into Clara's mouth in the park, the tiny fingers catching on her lip. He cried thinking of the child's unfocused blue eyes, and how they would only ever see that unreal landscape. For Clara, who had not spoken again about the pregnancy in all the weeks before they woke up in the city of impermanence. He cried for the impossibility of all of it.

Clara danced in the darkness of a nightclub not dissimilar to the one she had visited with Francis, her body sheened with sweat. She gathered her damp hair, tied it up carelessly. Arturo was a couple of steps in front of her, their friends surrounding them. He turned and smiled widely, elbowed through the tight crowd to get to her. He put his hands on her shoulders. Their friends put their arms around them. She was loved here, she remembered with astonishment.

Later that night, Clara kissed a tall stranger under the fluorescent light of a run-down lift, a friend of Arturo's. He smelled of woodsmoke and tobacco. They watched themselves kiss in the lift's mirror, as if watching strangers. He was not Francis. He was not an analogue for Francis's beloved body. She didn't know what he was. She felt alive, but not as alive as she felt walking home afterwards, alone, in the cold hour before dawn. The streets were so empty and so alien that she could almost pretend, for a moment, that she was back in the city of impermanence.

Francis, spooked, retreated to the knowable rhythms of the real world, and took new comfort in them. There was laundry to be sifted, there were carrots to be peeled, there were lectures to be given. *What next?* he thought, with panic, whenever he remembered the mysterious infant. For the first time, he did not find himself longing to return. He found himself afraid.

Arturo's friend came round to Clara's apartment the next evening. He was broad and quiet, and they sat for a long time on the sofa, talking softly in golden lamplight, before they moved to the bedroom that nobody else but Francis had seen in that way before. When she pressed her face into his neck she smelled woodsmoke still, and vetiver, and the clean edge of a soap she didn't know, and she rejoiced at its unfamiliarity.

He might actually fall for you. Be careful there, Arturo told her in the morning, after he had left. The three of them had had coffee together in their shared kitchen. Clara had thrilled with the ordinariness, with the relief of it.

I'm not doing anything, she said, and for a moment felt it almost true.

*

When Clara had discovered the pregnancy, the urge to see Francis had been too strong to suppress: her feet had carried her to his end of the city involuntarily. She didn't know which neighbourhood exactly was his, but to be in the vicinity felt enough – daring, hovering her hand over an electric wire. The test, with its two gentle pink lines, was in her pocket. Votive object. Proof of love.

If she was to see him, what would she do? she wondered. Would he be with his family? Would he look her right in the eye and ignore her, pretend they had never met? Would he be able to sense the change in her, the molecular alteration in her being? Would she discover his house, knock on the door and invite herself in, and with a few words detonate his life?

Anything felt possible. But if she detonated his life, he wouldn't love her any more, she remembered. Every thought was circular, looped back to this.

She dropped the test in a bin on the way home.

The day of the abortion she had been alone in her apartment, letting it happen. She ran a bath, let out the water, ran another. It was a weekend. Arturo was away. Francis and his family had gone to visit Iona's parents, and so he couldn't be with her; he had been apologetic but firm. It was the closest she had ever come to contacting him first, during those thin and terrible and stretched-out hours, where she went from one version of herself to another. Please, she had wanted to say. If you come and be with me now, here, I'll never ask another thing of you. But he had already become strange to her in the weeks since the pregnancy was discovered – remote, placing his hand on her still-flat stomach with trepidation, although fucking with the same hunger, as though nothing was really different, which she supposed it wasn't – and she was too afraid of pushing him away to break another rule.

But before the abortion, she had walked through the real city one day and found it remade.

Look at the sky, she had told their baby. Look at the pavement. Look at the beauty of this world, which is all for you.

The late-autumn leaves. The seasons repeating themselves. By then she could say to Francis, *This time last year, when we*. Attempts at solidity.

As she walked it became a city of memory, the years of versions of herself merging, filmy and overlaid.

At some point she walked past the hotel where they had lain on a bed during that gold-lit afternoon with the curtains drawn, a thunderstorm outside, and she felt such grief for the person she had been then. But she knew she had not been that person for a long time, anyway.

Francis was in pain. The wound on his foot seemed to be worsening, the skin around it reddening more each day, and the one on his wrist still hadn't healed. Both started to leak a faint yellow water. The pharmacist he went to was at a loss.

Have you encountered any allergens? he asked. Insect bites?

Not that I know of, Francis said.

The pharmacist prescribed him an antibiotic cream, which did nothing except sting.

Once could be a mistake, twice carelessness, but three sets something in motion, Clara thought to herself, as she once more found herself in the lift with the man who smelled like woodsmoke, who was not physically dissimilar to Francis, and who asked nothing of her.

I love another, she told him afterwards, when his arms were still around her, thinking of Arturo's words.

That's fine for now, he said. She listened to the sounds of the late-night traffic outside until he was asleep and then removed herself, gently, from his embrace.

Francis had felt the pregnancy keenly as both a betrayal of the unspoken erotic bargain they had made, and a betrayal of the domestic bargain he had more explicitly made elsewhere, and with everything balanced in such fragile symbiosis – dailiness and extraordinariness, secret and shown, the old love and the new – it was hard for him not to blame Clara for introducing this unexpected variable. It seemed better to pretend it had never happened.

Iona and Elise were still being wary with him, as if he were an impostor of sorts. If he tried to read her a story, Elise wouldn't concentrate. At bathtime, she threw a fit until they were both soaked. Sometimes he would catch Iona looking at him in a way that was difficult to parse, but which might have been contempt. He was afraid that it was contempt.

In the end, desire won out over fear. He knew he would return to Clara, given the option. He had started to long for her again, involuntarily. Her face swam before him in the night. He was between places, between lives, trapped outside of both. He may have to choose, he understood. Or the choice would be made for him. He didn't know which option scared him more.

Desire felt so pitiful to Clara that week. Paradise's bower revealed to be made of sticks and leaves, from whatever scraps were on offer. It had been an illusion. She could see clearly, she felt, more clearly than ever before. And it was bleak. How could something that felt so transcendent, so glorious, give away its own secrets in this way?

And yet.

Would I do anything to return? Clara thought, alone in her own kitchen. It was raining. The lights were turned off. Clara drank from her glass of red wine, watched the shape of the trees outside dancing in the wind. Her gaze followed their shadows where they fell against the wall. She slid down to the tiled floor so she could no longer see them, sat there with her knees pulled into her chest. *Yes*, she thought, sickened by her belief. She would still do anything to return.

Devotion

Clara blinked. She had not expected to be back in the city so soon. The whiplash of one place and then another. Sprawled on the bed, she couldn't move for a moment. When she got up and went to the window, the day's sky was marbled with grey. Francis remained asleep as she quietly, fruitlessly, searched for the baby in every room.

She put on a T-shirt, jeans and sandals, closing the front door carefully behind her. She kept expecting the invisible elastic that tied her to Francis to stall her feet, to trip her up, but the feeling didn't come. Outside, the air smelled ferrous, thick. There was a spot or two of rain. She walked towards their cafe on autopilot.

Francis woke with a jolt, veiled in sweat. He rose from the bed, calling hoarsely to Clara in the next room. Silence. He went to the bathroom and splashed his face, reached for his dressing gown. She would be making the coffee, he knew. Perhaps she was distracted, kitchen windows open, unable to hear him over the sound of the city.

But Clara was not in the kitchen. She wasn't in any of the rooms of the apartment. He checked them all several times, first baffled and then with rising panic. He dressed quickly and stumbled down the stairs, steered by instinct, almost falling, his hand reaching for the banister to steady himself. He was struck, suddenly, by the thought that she might be angry enough to leave him.

Clara sat at their usual table, under a ragged umbrella which flapped in the wind. She was calm. She could feel the tug inside her now, but only faintly. A cramping near her heart. The waitress came to take her order.

The usual, Clara said, smiling.

The waitress – a young girl with red curls – seemed nonplussed.

Did I miss your other? she asked, looking across to where her own partner, a boyish man with long dark hair, was taking someone else's order. Is he inside?

He's coming, said Clara.

Remind me of your usual? she asked.

The coffee was delivered without further comment, though the red-headed waitress crinkled her brow as she deposited it. Clara started to notice the other customers of the cafe casting her sideways glances. Two older men at the nearest table talked in low voices, looking at each other, then over at her. She downed her espresso, burnt, then left.

Francis moved rapidly through the dirty streets, trying to ignore the concerned looks of passers-by. He could sense Clara somewhere up ahead, knew that he was drawing nearer to her. Was that her – flash of dark hair, loose white T-shirt and old jeans, turning a corner? He recognized her because they were two parts of the same piece, they spoke without language, they had recognized each other from that first day at the museum. The despicable sentimentality of their mythology reared up in solace, in reminder, as he staggered around the corner, his pace quickening.

She was close, he really could sense it. Around the next corner, or the next. He could run a little easier now, his breathing less laboured. He almost barrelled into two short men in matching Hawaiian shirts, panted out an apology as he moved himself away from them. He kicked an empty tin out of his way with a surge of energy.

And there she was, he was sure of it. Clara! he shouted. The figure in the white T-shirt paused and turned around. It *was* her. He knew it. The terror in his chest abated so suddenly that he felt faintly ashamed of it.

She ran towards him, as if she had just remembered where she was. They embraced passionately, almost violently.

I'm sorry, she said, voice thick against his chest. I don't know what got into me. It just felt too strange to be there, today.

He nodded and squeezed her tighter, crushing her, his body's reassurance a kind of promise.

And yet underneath her relief she sensed a bruising, a spoiling of something. She recalled the emptiness of the city on their last visit, the day they had spent with the baby. A landscape of loneliness, the mythologies stripped of decoration and noise.

And her conscience whispered: *Well, yes. What else did you expect to find here?*

Adan and Lili's window had been dark for days. Clara looked in the morning, then before bed, but there was nothing.

Tourists, she thought, remembering Paula's words.

Still, it was uncanny to think of them vanished from this version of the city; the stark mausoleum of the cream leather furniture, the black marble table, all awaiting a return that might never come.

When Clara remembered the man who smelled of woodsmoke, she pushed him smoothly from her thoughts at once. He did not belong to the city of impermanence. *Containment*, she thought. But the next day she woke up and all the grass of the city had died, yellow and stark on the verges and in the parks, sharp under their hands.

It was thankless work, to sift such soil. They tried their best to bring green back to the park with loamy peat, with hoses and fertilizer, but nothing worked. It was no longer a pleasure to plant things in the stony earth, or to deadhead the desiccated flowers, and they spent most of their time picking up rubbish, broken glass and used condoms and plastic cups from the ruined ground.

Back to Paula and Jean's house in the early morning. Clara pulled Francis from the bed and he followed, half-asleep and unquestioning, and this time he was allowed into the room where everyone sat, every body soft, the remnants of the sleep they had so recently shared with the one they loved still upon them. Clara breathed, breathed, entered the landscape, feeling her way into it inch by inch.

But in the pale and formless place, Clara felt not euphoria but a profound sense of loss. The white light no longer seemed hazy but suggested, instead, an emptiness there could be no recovering from.

Afterwards, Francis didn't want to talk about what he had seen. I don't know if I did it right, he said, and Clara didn't push him.

Is it worth it? Clara asked herself, as they lay together on the bed, back at the apartment. It was not a question she allowed herself to ask often.

Has it been worth it?

To look at the question was like looking at a too-bright, dangerous light.

A visit to the museum. The journey took a long time, the train stuck in a tunnel for a reason that wasn't explained. Clara kept her hand, hot, in Francis's. She dug her nails in too hard to his palm, but he didn't complain. The lights went off, and then on again. A woman at the other end of the carriage was singing mournfully, as her companion, a spindly, tired-looking man, tried unsuccessfully to quieten her. An empty bottle rolled at their feet. Shut the fuck up! he shouted, and the woman hiccuped and fell silent. Clara glanced down towards them. The man's arm was around the woman. She was slumped low in the seat. The only other couple in the carriage was a pair of women in their late thirties, both with sharp blonde crops. They looked alarmed. One whispered in the ear of the other. Clara wondered if they had experienced the city in better days, or if this was the only iteration they knew. She tightened her grip on Francis.

When they reached the museum it was almost deserted. Someone had trodden leaves through the foyer. In wordless agreement, they headed towards the room where *Still Life with Cherries and Mouse* was displayed. There were many empty plinths on the way, the remaining exhibits in obvious disrepair. Clara felt sorry for the objects, abandoned, the glass cases cracked. Without witnesses, they lost their power.

It was dark in the final room, the main lights off. The only illumination came from the faint glow of the emergency lights in the ceiling. There was a high-pitched sound coming from somewhere. Even with the lights off, it was clear that the painting had changed. More bites missing from the apples, the artichoke petals plucked from their stems. The cherries mostly rotting to mulch, some stones left behind, spat out. The pewter jug on its side, spilling wine off the edge of the table, a suspended drop about to fall. Only crumbs were left of the bread, and smoke curled from the extinguished candle. Someone had sat at the table and eaten from it; someone had ransacked it, and then abandoned it. Clara couldn't tear her eyes away.

Francis eventually touched her, gently, on the elbow.

Let's go, he said.

Clara longed to be back in the museum where they had met: to be the version of herself with love, with love's possibility, all up ahead of her. A person about to take their first step into it.

What's the point? Francis asked one morning, as they prepared for work.

Please, Clara said simply.

When they arrived at the park he only stood and watched her as she continued with the small and now-meaningless tasks. Rain stippled the muddy water of the lake, on which ducks no longer bobbed. But there were still people boating, bedraggled, no champagne in sight. The argument they had had on the water was another lifetime ago. Pale fuzz coated the branches of the rose bushes. The larger trees leaked a sticky, rancid sap. Nobody else was turning up by then.

Another session with the devotionals. Paula had instructed them to fast beforehand. They had been in the shop buying milk when she told them. The milk sat, untouched, in the fridge. This session was deep in the night, deep in darkness. Clara's stomach was empty, her thoughts were pure, and the landscape continued to recede from her. She was conscious of Francis's body, warm next to her. Too conscious, perhaps, for she found she could not escape to wherever she needed to go; her focus tied, after all, so closely to his absence.

And yet these were the truest days of devotion, Clara thought. These days when the belief was shaken, and yet one still returned, and one still found joy. The days when you laid your neck down for love.

Devotion tested you. Perhaps it was not a technicolour city after all but a desert of pale sand, of milked-over sky, and that was what Paula's sessions were supposed to tell her. There was so much more of love to discover than the surface, which was easy and slippery and beautiful. Devotion, true devotion, was a vortex. It took, and it transformed. She tried hard to see it for what it really was. To give herself over to it.

*

A couple in the park set a small fire with all the kindling that was around. Clara spotted it before it did too much damage, just as the arsonists were running away. She screamed at them, waved her arms and pursued, running until she had no more breath.

Their bodies, oh their bodies; how grateful she was for their bodies and the language they continued to speak, when other language failed them.

He put his hands on her shoulders and pushed her gently, then not gently, to her knees. He leaned against the counter. She could not look away from him. He met her eyes, his hands in her hair, fingertips electric against her scalp. Clara, he said, almost disbelievingly, though they no longer had to use their names as proxies. Even then, even after everything, it was as if nobody had ever said her name before.

She had spent the morning making their favourite tart, apricot, and afterwards they ate slices of it, plated up with cream, curled on the bed.

Afterwards, afterwards. There was always an *afterwards*, when they returned to the world, whether impermanent or permanent, from the world of their bodies.

Clara was in the kitchen before bed, fetching a glass of water, when the lights finally came on again in Lili and Adan's apartment. She waited to see if anyone would come into view. The lights went off, and then back on. This time Lili walked into the living room. She moved slowly. Clara waved, but Lili either didn't see her or ignored her. She turned away from the window, bent down as if to pick up something, straightened and left the room, and when the lights went off they didn't come back on.

The next day, Clara watched and watched. It rained outside and Francis was fractious, a child kept inside, but Clara was stubborn.

They're there, she said. I need to see.

Eventually, in the early evening, the light came on again across the road. Lili and Adan were sat at the dinner table, facing one another.

I knew it, said Clara, triumphant. I knew they were back. I'm going to go and see them.

I'll stay, said Francis. There was a tremor in his voice that Clara chose to ignore.

You'll be all right, she said. I'll just be a moment.

She ran across the road, exhilarated — a gap in the traffic, the wind in her hair, alone for one moment, revelling in it, she realized with a sense of surprise and then disloyalty. The elastic to Francis stretched, the sensation mild and almost pleasurable, like working a muscle. Over the road, the door to the lobby was open again, and she ran up the stairs without pressing the buzzer, taking two at a time. The stairs of the building were dirty, some of the marble chipped, the bulbs blown. When she knocked there was no answer, though she could hear movement behind the door. She knocked again.

Hello! she called out.

The movement stopped. There was a long pause.

It's me, Clara tried. More movement, and then it stopped.

She hesitated, pressed her ear to the door. I just want to say hello, she tried.

Silence.

One morning Francis came back into the bedroom after his shower and found Clara in bed, reading the novel they both loved yet again, drinking coffee.

Where's mine? he asked.

I didn't make you any, she said, turning the page.

Hurt, he went through to the other room and rinsed out the pot, wiped spilled grounds from the counter. Was it cruelty? he wondered. Did that count as a harm?

But they didn't commit crimes against each other every day, not even crimes too minor to cross the threshold. Long periods of settled time could pass, or they seemed long anyway, in the fragile stretch of this new and common devotion.

Morning run, together, along the pedestrianized boulevards where the pavements were racked with potholes, where other couples still walked, holding hands. They turned into the smaller streets, winding and cramped with older buildings. In the heart of the city, the old town, things seemed to hold better. It was when the tight streets opened up, when they took turns that flung them unexpectedly into different architectural eras or landscapes, that strangeness started to make itself felt: more missing buildings with the squares of tarpaulin stretched tightly over their foundations, or buildings carelessly structured, lacking windows and stacked with bizarre, teetering extensions. Francis hurtled ahead, checked himself and slowed, looking over his shoulder at Clara. She pushed herself and caught up with him, then overtook him and did not look back.

She showered alone afterwards, standing up in the bathtub behind the rapidly mildewing yellow curtain, the water almost unbearably hot. She loved Francis. She had betrayed Francis. She had not loved herself, but she had betrayed herself also, anyway, throughout her entire life.

She watched the water drain slowly down the plughole.

One day she would wake up, and her life would be gone without her even realizing. Lived one foot in and one foot out.

And she came out wet and angry and ashamed, her hair in a towel, and Francis smiled at her with such softness, and the voice in her head became at once silken, toothless.

You love him. Nothing is perfect. Don't ruin what you have been given.

There will be nothing in your life that ever feels like this again.

Anger evaporated, leaving a feeling lingering in its wake that she spent the rest of the day trying to name. Before they fell asleep – no longer doing so entwined by then, but still comfortable, back to back, the lines of their bodies aligned – she placed it, finally, as homesickness.

Clara's skin prickled. Francis's hand was on the pillow, next to her face. She studied her own ring, the opal where it glimmered. Then she studied the gleam of Francis's in the morning's light, before touching it lightly.

Going very slowly, she started to twist the wedding ring. She froze when he shifted, seeming to get close to awakening. When he was motionless again, she gave it another try.

Francis was not asleep; he had woken as soon as she had touched him, and he wasn't sure why he was pretending. Clara pawing at the ring felt both absurd and strangely arousing. He took a kind of pleasure in the knowledge she would not be able to remove it, and in how she had given in to her urge to try.

I would like to cut it off, she thought, dreamlike, of the cold metal, of his finger.

She was getting frustrated, he could tell. Her movements grew less careful. She was hurting him. He pretended to wake up, gradually, faking a yawn.

What are you doing? he asked, expecting her to be embarrassed, but she continued. Now she was really hurting him, and she must have known, though he tried not to show it.

It's stuck, she said, throwing his throbbing hand down on to the bed.

Her cheeks were flushed with the effort. Her eyes, alert, watched him. He lifted his left hand and ran it down the curve of her torso, exposed and languid among the thrown-off sheets. He took her own hand with it, and placed it on his body.

As she touched him, the man who smelled like woodsmoke came to her mind, and before she could push the thought away Francis let out a shout, shrinking away from her.

Was that static? I felt a shock, he said. Did you feel that?

Outside it started to rain, very hard, out of nowhere. The downpour was so heavy that they ran to the window. It was like a bucket being emptied. It lasted for one minute, two maybe, and then stopped as suddenly as it had started.

Clara confessed at a farmers' market as they shopped for dinner, over a display of ripe tomatoes, unable to hold in her secret any longer.

I fucked someone else.

It was noisy, and at first Francis thought he had misheard her.

What? he asked distractedly, picking up a paper bag.

I fucked someone else, Clara enunciated. It felt surprisingly satisfying to say it. Francis put the bag down and looked at her.

When?

The last time we were in the real city, she said.

Oh, he said. Right.

He picked up the bag again and placed a few tomatoes in it, then walked to the counter to weigh and pay for them, handing over the money. Clara remained, watching him.

I'm sorry, she said, when he returned.

You're always sorry, he said.

They walked together past the stalls of cheeses, of pastries, of fruits. Clara picked up a cube of stale bread from a dish and dipped it in oil.

As if you haven't fucked other people too, she said.

Yes, sometimes I sleep with Iona, he said. We're married.

No, she said. I mean the others.

There are no others, he said.

Clara laughed.

Not for years, he said. Not since long before you.

They were silent as they walked, reaching the end of the row. Clara examined some tiny green apples.

What makes me different from all the ones before me? she asked.

I love you, he said. I didn't love them.

You make it sound so simple, she said. She picked up four apples and put them in a bag. She held out her hand to Francis for a coin.

Because it is, he replied, giving one to her.

She handed it over to the stallholder.

This isn't just an affair to me, she said. This is it. The big love story.

The stallholders looked away.

What makes you think it's not the same for me? he asked.

The fact that we're here, rather than *there*, she said.

And he found he had no answer for this.

He was silent as they walked. Clara kept looking at him out of the corner of her eye. They stopped at another stall for hot chocolate in takeaway cups. Clara asked for brandy in hers. Francis wanted to comment, but didn't. He felt cold all over.

They left the market, cutting through an alley and emerging into another square, much smaller, with benches on each side facing the circular fountain at its centre. They stopped and sat.

So, do you do this often? he asked eventually. This fucking of people who aren't me.

No, she said. I'm mostly true to you.

Mostly, he said. He laughed a short, sharp laugh.

You have a family, she said. You have an entire life.

So you decided to punish me for things I can't change, things I have never hidden from you, he said. You punish me, and you punish yourself.

His voice was measured. He lifted his chocolate to his lips, then changed his mind and put the cup down on the floor next to the bench.

Do you regret it? he asked.

Clara considered.

No, she said.

He looked up towards the smooth sky.

The pointlessness of it all, he said.

She turned to him.

You were the one who told me I shouldn't put myself in a waiting room, she said.

I didn't want to make any demands of you, he said. But obviously I didn't mean this. I thought you understood.

Love requires demands, she retaliated. Maybe I wanted you to make them! And maybe then I would have respected them.

I very much doubt you would have, he replied.

He stood up abruptly and started to walk across the square. Clara's face was hot. She felt the words rise in her throat like they were being pulled out of her by the invisible elastic, stretching, stretching.

I wish I had never met you! she shouted after him. I wish I was free to live a normal life!

Francis paused, then turned around.

You don't mean that, he said.

I do.

He opened his arms theatrically, sweeping the square. Well, you're absolutely free to go, Clara! Don't let me stop you!

She blinked, tears welling.

Go back! Go back and fuck someone else! Go back and fuck the entire population of the real world, see if I care. You evidently have no control over yourself, and no concept of loyalty whatsoever.

He pointed at her. She felt it like a physical blow.

And you know what's really funny? I always knew these things about you, and for some reason I thought you would change. But you never will, because you're totally incapable of thinking about anyone but yourself.

Oh, and you're so perfect, with your beautiful fucking family and your sordid little midlife crisis! A model of self-control and loyalty, right? Clara's voice was hoarse. I would never do to you what you've done to me, keeping me a secret for all this time, stringing me along!

Francis shook his head. I've made no promises.

She set her own cup down on the bench and stood. You never loved me.

I've loved you much more than you deserve!

Are you joking? You think I deserve less than this? Even less than this?

Clara stepped forward to face him, the way she had on the first morning in the city of impermanence, like they were two strangers duelling. Francis held up his hand.

Don't come near me, he said.

I have to! I physically have to!

Walk behind me, then, he said, turning around.

The other couples were watching them openly.

Oh, piss off! Clara yelled at them as if they were seagulls, waving her arm around ineffectually, and most dropped their gaze. Blood dripped to the ground from the new wound on her forearm.

In the apartment, she stood a little distance away from Francis. His shoulders were slumped, back turned to her.

I'm sorry, she tried again, the words feeling strange in her mouth.

Me too, he said eventually. What a scene.

Wet faces, then, and the urgent motion of their limbs. Their bodies forgave each other first.

I didn't mean it, Clara said afterwards, exhausted, as they lay on the bed. I didn't mean any of those things.

Francis stroked her hair.

It meant nothing, she said.

Let's forget it, he said.

He inspected every inch of her skin, as if looking for ticks. She was very still under his hands. The body of one who had betrayed him. The freckles at her shoulder, the blue veins at the back of her knees, the blisters on her toes, the bruised shins, all examined with forensic patience. Someone else had seen these things. A tiny flare of disgust that he brushed aside. Instead he noticed each blemish and imperfection and forgave them, unasked, in a way that felt selfless, marvelling at pale scar tissue, at the history of herself as left on herself. Her palm, sliced by a broken wine glass. Her knee, where she had fallen hard as a child on to gravel, a speck of dirt still visible under the surface if you looked very closely. Her eyebrow, bisected by a short white line, where she had knocked her head, drunk, years before they had met. When she appeared in a hotel room with a new mark or bruise, he would think about all the life happening to and around her that he didn't see, that he didn't know, with a kind of amazement.

He was a hypocrite, he knew, remembering his family, remembering how close he had come to kissing the waitress. But he hadn't kissed her. And Clara had known the situation from the start. And yet someone else had laid a hand here, and a hand there. Her skin was smooth, obedient. He could almost feel her blood beating through the surface.

The wounds left by the city of impermanence had healed. There was only the new one on her arm, a shallow, round sore a little bigger than a largish coin. He had one too, on the corresponding arm. He bandaged hers and then she bandaged his, gently. She kissed the soft skin just below his elbow.

They stayed awake for as long as they could in order to delay their departure, pacing around the room, leaning out of the window and into the cold air, slapping their arms. But even as they moved, their eyes grew unbearably heavy. Their heads and limbs swayed, as if drunk.

I don't want to go, she said.
I know, he said. Me neither.
I'll miss you.
Come back soon.
Only if you do, she said.
And then nothing.

Return

Francis woke up into his life. It was very early. He went to Elise's room. There she was, still asleep, the knitted elephant she took to bed each night fallen to the floor. Automatically, he picked it up and positioned it on the nightstand next to her bed, sitting it up, as if waiting for her to barrel into the day. He was a father, he remembered. He was a father and a husband. The idea felt less real than the idea of the city of impermanence. He was a father and a husband and a liar, he remembered, as if for the first time. He was irredeemably those three things.

Clara attended to herself with care, during those days of return. She ate three square meals a day and read in the tentative warmth of the park, stretched out on a blanket, went to bed early. For the first time, the ring had travelled back with her from the city. The stone seemed chipped, the metal dull. It came off her finger easily; she put it in the drawer next to her bed, nestled with the key card from the hotel, so it wouldn't be lost.

She tried to settle inside her life. Tried to imagine how it would feel not to have one foot outside its outline, always dreaming of elsewhere. Tried to remember how it had felt to brush up against the real, the allowable body of the man who smelled of woodsmoke. Presence over absence. Easy presence.

*

Francis fell sick, a burning-up on re-entry. He lay in bed with a fever for several days. Iona cared for him without complaint, bringing him soup, bringing him Elise, who heaped her toys on the bed and stuck a sticky fake thermometer in his mouth. He was lucky, he knew. To be shown such compassion.

He drank water straight from the tap in the bathroom, and then stuck his head under the tap too. He peeled back the bandage to stare at the last wound. He dreamed fever-dreams of Clara, that she was in the room watching him, shadowy, from the doorway. In the dreams, he waved her away in fear.

What will happen to the city when it's all over? Clara thought a few days later. *What will I remember of my time there, if the end comes?*

Was the city of impermanence life itself, distilled to its purest pleasures, or reprieve from life? Was it a city of impasse, a city of impossibility? Purgatory, or state of grace?

Clara didn't know what she would remember, or what she would want to remember. She didn't know how she would tell it to herself, or to others.

What did he look like, the man she had betrayed him for? That man was in the city somewhere, Francis knew. Perhaps he was with Clara right at that moment. It made him feel sick.

Sometimes I wonder where you go, Iona said, next to him in the kitchen. She was chopping the vegetables. He was browning the meat.

What do you mean?

There was a pause. Putting down the knife, she came to him and put her hands on his face. Scrutinized him closely, as if some answer could be found in the lines around his eyes, in the curl of his lips. He held her gaze with difficulty.

Whatever's going on with you, you need to figure it out, she said. She dropped her hands, turned away.

I don't know what you mean, he said again. He touched the top of her shoulder, tentatively. She felt more fragile than he remembered through her soft black jumper.

Come on, she said, moving from his grasp. Neither of us are idiots.

She returned to her chopping.

Do you want to be here? she asked over the staccato of the knife, tone controlled, neutral.

Francis saw the opportunity hovering.

Of course, he said, hating himself.

The opportunity vanished as if it had never been there.

Maybe start acting like it, then, she said.

He took his pan off the heat, defiant.

I'm going to check on Elise, he said.

Yes, she said. Go and see your daughter.

Clara took long walks along the canal, alone or with friends. They stopped at beer gardens to sit and watch the world go by. Summer was approaching. When it arrived it would mark six months since the city of impermanence opened to her, two years she had been following Francis wherever he would take her. She licked the sweat from her top lip, felt it gather under her arms. Here were her hands, smoothing her skirt along her thighs, twisting her hair over her shoulder. Here were her feet, rubbing against her sandals. Here was the world in all its glorious imperfection. The sunsets were lingering, radiant, announced nothing. The grass browned, then greened again. Little had changed in her absence. The real city didn't need her belief, or punish her when it faltered. The real city forgave everything.

*

Francis took the train into the centre of the city, and in the museum of gilt-framed paintings he went straight away to *Still Life with Cherries and Mouse*. It looked smaller, after all the iterations he had known over the last months. He had relived that first day when he followed her around in the real world so many times that he felt mournful for how the memory must have been, unavoidably, warped; buffed to a softer shine, parts misremembered, though he had tried so hard to fix it in his mind. He tried to call up a previous version of Clara, willed her to walk into the room.

He moved through the rest of the museum with the feeling that she was out of sight, fleeting, just around the next turn. If he moved fast enough, he might be able to find her.

But he was there alone, he accepted finally, once every room had been visited. She had betrayed him. He should not have come. Now the museum would always contain the possibility, the ghost, of a Clara who had betrayed him. Like this, everything would be ruined – slowly, but precisely. In the bathroom he locked himself in a toilet cubicle and cried for a moment, a sharp, clean shiver of grief, before leaving to go home.

Clara sat at her desk in the gallery and tried to make herself as still as possible, as if meditating. She was passing the time. She was considering her next move. The air conditioning was cold above her head. She hated herself. She had betrayed him. She hated herself for betraying him.

From the window of her crowded bus to work that morning, she had felt certain that she glimpsed him on the street – the strong profile of his face, tanned arm emerging from a clean white T-shirt – and she had rung the bell to get off early, but when she had emerged on to the pavement, breathless, deranged, she found it was not him at all but an impostor, younger and swaggering and looking at her askance. She had stared at him until he swung around and continued on to wherever he was going.

I would do anything to return. I would do anything to return.

Her gallery was not far from the museum where *Still Life with Cherries and Mouse* was located. When the gallery closed early, on her half-day, she walked over to it. She had the superstitious, hopeful feeling that she would see Francis, though she knew rationally that he must be working, with students or sitting in some departmental meeting. The museum was very quiet. She waited in front of their painting, her thoughts cool and slight, trying to empty herself so that something else might fill the space.

He wasn't there. He might never be there again, she realized, moving out into the street, a wall of heat and people. Their voices were overwhelming, and nobody was him.

Francis dreamed of colour and coldness and found on waking that Iona was staring at the ceiling, already awake, thinking her own untraversable thoughts. And he felt closer to her, both lost in their own private mysteries, than he had for a long time.

Clara drew fat moons, lonely coasts, votive objects. She sat outside her apartment, on the steps, and drew the people who walked past. She drew Francis from memory, after all. She could call him up with such detail, it was like he was actually there.

She longed for his touch, her body an instrument in the sunlight. Later she touched herself thinking only of his hands. She did not see the man who smelled like woodsmoke. It was too little, too late, she knew, as an atonement.

*

Francis in the paddling pool, with Elise, the summer upon them. Iona watched them from the shade, blue-striped bikini, a book on her lap. She smiled. What did she see, these days, when she looked at him? he wondered. Could he still be an object of desire? He lifted the extraordinary proof of their previous desire upside down, shook her until she shrieked. Or did seeing him like this, in the context of what their desire had made, strip him, somehow, of the status of object? In the bathroom upstairs, still damp from the pool, he tried to see his body how Clara saw it, to remember how hungrily she always looked and touched, for he was forgetting, he feared, and he wanted to hold tight to every detail, but time was relentless that year, and he felt powerless to halt the days that took her further away from him.

Arturo and Clara went to the seaside. Cans of beer in translucent blue plastic bags for the train journey, sand to sprawl on when they arrived under sweltering sky. They ran into the sea, drunk, and ran back out, fell asleep on their towels, woke to pinkened skin. Fish and chips, more sea, more beer, a shaded pub garden, new friends, a walk up to a secret beauty spot, Clara limping in her flip-flops, emerging over the top of dunes and beachgrass to see the molten disc of the sun hitting water. Running for the train home, nearly missing it. A good day. One of the best, she thought, before falling asleep, sunburnt, on Arturo's shoulder. The kind of day to keep you in your life.

I miss you, Francis mouthed as he stood in the garden at dusk, the paddling pool abandoned and the air thick with the scent of honeysuckle, wondering if there was a way she would hear, would sense it.

*

Autumn started to draw in and Clara waited, even as the days passed, even as she found ways to fill them. The gallery was busier; the polystyrene-and-wire sculptures that she had hated so much had been an unexpected success. Now there were press queries to field, portfolios left on her desk by her manager, a steady flow of visitors. Sometimes she went to the library and picked books indiscriminately, reading them among the strangers reading at long wooden desks carved with the initials of people long since gone. She went with the girl in the leather coat from her friend's show to another exhibition, then to the theatre. She had forgotten that the girl was good company, observant and dry, and almost found herself confessing to her situation with Francis, as they debriefed over murky glasses of ale in an ancient pub near the theatre. What's your story? the girl asked. What's going on with your heart? And Clara had wavered, she had ached, but she had not given herself away. There were dinners where she sat, quietly, next to Arturo as he presided over wine stains on the tablecloths, dripping candlewax, and then the emerging together into a night sky that smelled of smoke and rain, not minding that she had barely said anything. She felt a new kind of awake. She was not unhappy.

They never bumped into the man she had betrayed Francis with. She still did not know his last name, the same way Francis had not known hers that first time they slept together, the room in the shared house, the afternoon light thick with dust.

In that room she had transfigured the sordid into the beautiful by pure force of will. Now she had transfigured it back.

In hope's slow absence, her life started to fold around her more gently. She wondered about travelling somewhere. A new city, another country, another life to try on.

One morning when she woke, too half-asleep to put up a real fight, the voice in her head said: *Living in longing for so long did not give you happiness.*

It felt like happiness, Clara argued. At least some of the time.

It was not happiness, said the voice.

One cold night Clara walked home in the dark and a song started playing in her headphones, one she used to play in the hours and days after seeing Francis, and her heart swelled in muscle memory. *I would do anything to return.*

Francis sat in his tiny office with the lights off after everyone else had left, the industrial cleaning machines roaring up and down the corridors outside, and thought for the thousandth time, *She betrayed me*; and thought, *It will never be the same again*; and thought, *Yet I would still do anything to return.*

The Dinner

Bright light. The cotton of the bed crisp, new. They turned to each other as if it were the first time.

    It's not always possible to recognize the last thing when it happens, especially when all evidence points to the contrary. It was summer again, the sun so hot, pouring itself on to the parquet with joyful vehemence. The apartment must have been refurbished, everything spotless, the floor shining and unmarked. In the other room, though they couldn't see it, the shelves were full of books, all their favourites, books they had recommended to each other or read at the same time. Neither of them spoke. Neither wanted to break the silence. On the wall behind the velvet sofa was a framed print of *Still Life with Cherries and Mouse*.

Hearing noise from outside, Clara and Francis went, naked, to the French windows of the balcony. A large parade filled the street below, a brass band moving in unison, its music muffled through the glass, the paired players clad in uniforms of red and yellow. People standing on the sidelines were subsumed into the crowd, handed musical instruments and brightly coloured paper streamers – couple after couple after couple, old and young, well matched and ill matched, couples temporarily parted by the crowd, and then coming, laughingly, back together. Clara took the sheet from the bed and wrapped it around herself, opened the door and stepped out on to the balcony, watching all the people snaking below, faces looking up to her, and Francis beside her now, the crowds stretching out their hands. Come down! they shouted. Clara saw Paula and Jean, blue circles painted on their cheeks and streamers draped around their shoulders, and waved.

They dressed with childlike, hushed excitement. Feet quick on the marble staircase, and Francis watched Clara stepping so easily ahead of him, moving in the ways that made all else around her ridiculous, and he could have watched her all day, but there was no time for that, already they had reached the door that would lead them into the street and into the crowd. They emerged into the sunlight, the swell of bodies, moving two by two. All these people, who had created a world from their own belief. They had never really been alone.

The parade carried them through the neighbourhood. They passed their favourite cafe, the one which had vanished months ago, and the restaurant where they had eaten on their first night, and the fountain was brimming with coins, more gold than water. More and more people joined on every street, drawn by the noise, the whistles and the music. Someone handed Clara a can of beer, which she drank thirstily, despite the early hour, sharing it with Francis. It tasted sour. The crowd was boisterous, unknown figures knocking into Clara so that she dropped the can, held on to Francis's hand, tight, anticipation curling in her chest. His hand was warm, solid. Remember this, she told herself, the way she had told herself so many times before.

They reached the edge of the old town and kept going, moving into the district where glass towers pushed up into the hard blue sky. The crowd flowed around the gaps in the city's architecture without pausing, tarpaulin squares stretched out on the ground. Some sites were being rebuilt, scaffolding and plastic half-constructed, but nobody seemed to be working on them. Clara had not seen a single construction worker. It must happen at night, she thought, when the objects in the museum are moved around by unknown hands, and the passage between cities slips, quietly, open.

They passed the museum. People ran out of the front door

to join the carnival, leaping down the steps, almost stumbling in their eagerness. They passed through Paula and Jean's neighbourhood, the well-tended lawns, the neat cottages, their front doors opening and residents coming out, hand in hand, and the parade was still driving them on, into the outskirts of the city now, empty industrial lots, the warehouse club they had visited with Lili and Adan – Clara looked for them in the crowd but all the faces blurred together as they danced past – and then they were at the edge, past the edge, the concrete giving way to red dirt, and then to sand beneath their feet.

As they approached the shoreline, the crowd sprawled. Some people broke off and sat down. Others stood, looking out over the water. Others still walked right into the surf, rolling up trousers, hitching up dresses. They shrieked at the cold, splashed each other. Above them on the shore, the brass band played on.

You want this, Clara told herself.

You no longer want this, she told herself.

She didn't want to look at Francis. Her happiness all at once was fragile, teetering. But what was she afraid of? Under the blue, the sweltering sun, there was nothing sinister in the landscape. She slipped off her shoes and left them where they fell. She walked towards the water, tiny sharp stones digging into the soles of her feet. When she reached the water, it took her breath away. She had the urge to swim to the horizon. She did not look back to see if Francis was following.

They left the crowd on the shore and walked back into the city. It was quiet. Clara felt the memory of recent joy in her chest, an imprint like a thumb pressed into clay.

At their cafe, their usual table was free, the one closest to the fountain. There was only one other couple there, everybody else presumably still at the beach. The red-haired waitress was excitable. Did you see the parade? Wasn't it fun?

Clara ordered a large meal for both of them: coffee, orange juice, omelettes and toast and pieces of a dense, fruited cake, buttered. She felt starving and ate quickly. Francis watched her.

You've always had such a good appetite, he said, speaking for the first time that day. She didn't respond right away.

We were gone for a long time, she said eventually.

We were, he said. I missed you.

Clara looked away.

I went to see our painting, she said. In the real world. It's stupid, but I thought maybe you would be there too. That somehow you would find me there, the way you found me the first time.

I went to see it too, said Francis. I thought the same. But you weren't there.

His eyes were softer than she had ever seen them before.

I have missed you so much, she said. I almost miss you now.

I'm here, said Francis. He took her hand and leaned forward, placed it on his chest. She could feel his heart beating under the thin cotton of his T-shirt — skittish, full.

She thought about the seconds before she would answer the door to him in the real world; how the affair had compressed her life into moments of unbearable vibrancy, the brightness of them. The truth of them. Maybe it was in absence that they loved each other best, and most honestly.

Yet his heart beat under her hand, present and undeniable. She looked into his eyes and he met her gaze steadily.

She took her hand away when the waitress came back, ordered another coffee. Then she wanted a cigarette, and so she had one. Francis took it off her halfway through and inhaled, his eyes closed.

Tastes like twenty years ago, he said. Time travel.

Clara touched the dead petals of the rose in its blue vase.

Would you have done anything differently? she asked.

Francis exhaled a long plume of smoke, opened his eyes.

No, he said. I would make the same unforgivable mistakes all over again.

They walked east, towards the park on the hill overlooking the city. It was further away than either of them had remembered, and when they arrived it was crowded with people still wearing their face paint, paper streamers tangled in their hair. They found a place to sit.

The sun was about to set. She sensed everybody waiting, anticipating. The darkness started to fall as it always did, the familiar fade of pink and deep blue, and she clicked her fingers as it switched, the unfurling of night against day. It wasn't real, she understood. It was possible that none of it had been real.

Francis was quiet. He was lying down now, lit by the residual glow of twilight. His T-shirt was rucked up, exposing three inches of flat stomach, tenderly furred. Clara put out her hand to it and felt the muscles tense. She clarified her thoughts. Some things had been real.

Clara had done her best to memorize Francis in the real world, during the times they spent together. She scanned the length of him now, slowly, taking in the impossible density of his presence. She didn't want to miss anything, to forget anything. His legs, askew on the grass. His wide shoulders, his large hands, always his hands.

Fine, easy enough to remember his hands – which touched her, which held her, which she held in turn – but then what of the subtler details? The curve of his collarbone, which she loved to run her fingers along; the raised mole near his navel, the pale appendix scar carved near his hipbone, the birthmark at the nape of his neck?

And what of his rare and boyish laugh, his attention to the detail of all things, the way he closed his eyes in pleasure in the sun, the long and easy stride of his walk? She had always tried to reduce him to parts, but in the end she had never truly managed it. He was only, in the end, himself. An object beloved, ungraspable, most beautiful in entirety.

How she loved him. How she had loved him. How she believed, and continued to believe, despite it all.

He sat up and looked towards the city's vista, starting to glitter with evening lights.

Let's go for dinner, he said.

They changed in the apartment, Francis helping Clara fasten the short yellow lacework dress as she lifted up the curtain of her hair. Cool breeze at her neck from the balcony door, left ajar. Then it was her turn to button his shirt, to straighten his collar. He stood unmoving under the quick motions of her hands. While they were still dressing, the lights in the apartment went out. She froze for a moment, unsure, and he went to try the light switch, but it had stopped working. They walked carefully down the staircase in the dark, out into the street.

The streets bore the remnants of the morning's festivities: paper streamers, crumpled cans and broken glass. As they walked, there was a low roll of thunder in the distance. It started to rain. They walked faster, and the rain kept coming, falling harder until they broke into a run, the dye from the streamers bleeding on to the paving stones around them.

Clara laughed breathlessly. By the time they arrived at the first restaurant they had ever visited in the city of impermanence, her hair hung loose and wet around her shoulders, and their clothes were heavy with water. It didn't matter.

Inside, then. They were seated at the back, at a table too big for two. The same starched white tablecloth as before, the same red ashtray. A tall, sallow candle in a pewter holder. There was nobody else dining. Clara and Francis waited in silence, looking at each other.

A waiter arrived with two glasses of red wine and almonds, salted, in a small white bowl. Clara put an almond on her palm and examined it, before slipping it into her mouth. She looked across to his beautiful solemn face, watching her intently.

I'll never really have you, will I? she asked.

She picked up another almond.

But you do have me, Francis said. You have me here, in all the best ways.

What if I want the other ways?

Francis looked at the floor. He seemed disappointed in her.

Let's not do this now, he said, as usual.

No, she said. Let's do it now. When else?

Francis was silent for a moment.

Something was coming to her, some memory unfurling. She pictured herself as if from a great height.

A hotel lift, Clara standing alone under amber light, surveying her reflection, the flare of her pupils. Then walking down a dark-carpeted, windowless corridor. Her fist lifted to knock against a door, behind which Francis waited.

The corridor, the knock, the hotel bed where all was permitted and Francis upon it. All in place, all as she had willed it. But this time, a crisis. Not a new crisis but a deepening one, one no longer able to be deferred, not after the proof of love, the path not taken and not even considered. She had changed, and he had not noticed, or wanted to notice. The words coming out of her mouth still felt like a surprise to her. She still did not want to say them.

Don't go, was all that Francis offered in response.

But she did go. For the first time in their relationship, she left.

I was leaving you, Clara said in the restaurant. Before we woke up here. Do you remember it too?

I don't remember, he said.

He didn't want to remember.

Try, she said.

He closed his eyes.

In the hotel room, Clara disappearing through the doorway, and Francis failing to follow. Instead he stayed until it was time for checkout, expecting her to return, then not expecting it. He let the dregs of the champagne go warm and flat in their glasses. He touched nothing, as if preserving a crime scene. As if love could be simply stepped back into.

Come back to me, he thought.

I should have followed her, he thought.

But it was too late.

And then he put his head in his hands, and then he dressed and tidied the room, stepped from wet pavement into a taxi, watched the city pass from the window as he returned to his home.

Yes, he said, opening his eyes again. I remember. But it doesn't matter. I know you didn't mean it. You were frustrated. I can understand.

He grasped across the table for Clara's limp hand.

And we're here now, aren't we? Somehow, we have been given the gift of this place.

He gestured at the room around them. Clara took it all in. The two waiters, moving smoothly through their tasks. The rain visible through the window, heavier than before. The love songs on the speakers, so familiar now that she knew every word.

But it isn't real, she said.

The volume of the music wavered up suddenly, then down.

All this talk of what's *real*. When there's so little for you in the real world, Francis said decisively. He let go of her hand, pushed his chair back as if to distance himself from her.

Clara felt winded. Is that really what you think?

It's what you tell me all the time, he said.

She looked at him steadily.

You've hurt me, she said, simply.

And you've hurt me, he retorted at once. Isn't that how every love story goes?

What happened to the great romantic?

The realization that you always end up in the same place, after all.

The waiter came back, bearing more food they hadn't ordered: two artichokes, purple and green and flourishing; a small dish of a pale yellow sauce.

I don't want to be here any more, Clara said.

Francis stared at her. She had spoken so quietly that, for a moment, he thought he must have misheard. She met his eyes just before the lights went out across the restaurant, the way they had done in the apartment earlier. He blinked, and gradually the contours of her face came back into focus, flickering in the candlelight.

Clara. My love. You don't mean that, he said.

She plucked an artichoke leaf and dipped it in the sauce, sucked its fruit from the stem. Outside, the square was deserted. The street lamps had gone out too, she realized. Perhaps it was a city-wide power cut. She stared at the water streaming down the windows.

You've put me in a waiting room, she said. This is a waiting room.

No, he said. This is a paradise. Our paradise.

He let out a long breath and put his head into his hands. She watched his body fold lower, towards the table.

A crash of crockery came from the kitchen. The song started to skip over the speakers, stuck on the word *you you you*, and Clara looked at Francis and thought *you*, thought with terror of never seeing him again, of never returning to the city of impermanence, the eye-watering blue and the objects in perpetuity, where everything changed but nothing changed meaningfully, where they would go over the same ground again and again and again. She thought, with a new terror, of being trapped in this city for ever.

The waiter was back again. Butter, smooth and golden, a whole dish of it. Francis cut slices of bread with the silver breadknife. His hands were trembling.

I love you, said Clara. I still love you.

So why leave? said Francis.

Because you won't give me anything real, she said.

I've given you all I could, he replied.

Clara knew both statements had their own truth. It depended on the angle you viewed them from, the light, the time of day.

Please don't go, he said. He leaned forward. His face was open, beseeching, in a way she had never seen before.

We can't stay here for ever, that's true, but we can promise always to come back. We can fall asleep next to each other at night and wake up next to each other in the morning. Even if we're sometimes apart – no one's ever with the person they love all the time, anyway, and we can miss each other, we can wait to return to this place the way we would any beloved place, like a holiday in your favourite country. A home away from home. It doesn't have to be all one way or another, does it? It hasn't been perfect, I know. Nothing ever is. But can't we forgive each other? Don't we deserve some mercy, some happiness?

The waiter appeared to clear the table, then set down a plate of apple slices and cherries, burnished and shining. They ate them in silence, until their fingers were stained red with the juice.

When they left the restaurant, the fountain outside was in ruins. It had crumbled spectacularly in the short time they had been inside. Dust and coins were all that remained. As they passed it, the ground beneath them shuddered, a sudden movement that almost knocked them over. Francis clutched at Clara, then let go of her quickly, as if ashamed.

As they walked home the city fell around them, a swift and brutal razing. The leaves withered on the trees. The pavement cracked, red earth showing beneath. There was nobody else to be seen. It seemed that the city, in its destruction, was all theirs again.

They arrived back at the apartment and stood in the kitchen, facing each other. The lights were still out. Francis found candles and lit them as Clara remained motionless. He came to her and took her face in his hands.

Tell me you really want to leave, he said. Say it.

You want what is real, the voice in her head spoke loudly, insistent as a heartbeat.

And yet there will never be anything better than this, it countered itself.

But what if there could be something truer, something not yet imagined?

Clara put her arms around him. I want to leave, she said. I am leaving.

His hands dropped but she held on to him, and he yielded, the faint smell of jasmine soap from his neck, the solid shape of him, a body already lost to her, like the void left by a collapsing star.

Eventually they lay down on the floorboards, side by side, no longer touching. Clara was shaking. A sudden musical clatter as a pane of glass from the balcony door blew in, then a second one. Francis sat up and surveyed the damage, then lay back down. Sharp pain in the palm of Clara's hand. She lifted it above their faces. Francis caught her wrist and examined the small red wound, right in the centre. A drop of blood trickled slowly down her arm. He let go.

It's the end, he said.

Love was picking up the same old tune and embellishing. It was nothing new. They had invented nothing, even if it felt like they had. Love was a fiction that the other person interpreted differently. The story that she had lived had felt true, but it was not the story that Francis had lived. Clara told herself this over and over, trying to make herself a nonbeliever. It had all been done before and would be done again.

But it was impossible to quantify how it had felt to wake up next to him on the first morning, as if everything in her life had been leading to it. As if everything she had denied herself, everything she had set aside, everything she had ignored or looked away from or pretended not to know, had finally borne fruit.

Hairline fractures webbed the ceiling's plaster even as they looked up. The rain was coming in. It scattered over their bodies. Clara closed her eyes. She felt no relief. Instead she was struck both by panic and by an irresistible exhaustion.

No, she said out loud. No, she told the city.

She wasn't ready, but then she would never be ready. Francis pressed his mouth to hers, urgently, as if it could keep them there. She clutched for him. But she was already gone.

Permanence

Clara finds herself in the museum, her feet moving as if of their own volition. A little over a decade has passed since she met a stranger there, since they crossed a line together. Perhaps Francis has been here without her in the meantime. Perhaps he is in another city, another country, even. The possibilities no longer feel violent, though each one is plausible.

It's quiet today. No rain; it's clear and cold. The chill from outside hangs on her wool coat. She goes slowly so as not to startle him, or the ghost of him. Soon she will be the same age he was when they first met. The years in her body, crowded, settling into place.

The cool metal of his wedding band touched her face, and like that – transformation. Symbolic object, forbidden object, a deal brokered. She didn't know what she was setting in motion. All she knew was that when she left the museum the world was washed clean, as brightly as if dipped in oil or water.

For a long time she waited to wake up back in the city, fearing it and longing for it alternately. But each morning she opened her eyes and found herself still living in a state of permanence.

She used to worry that without him she would feel nothing at all, as if he were the voltage that gave the world itself its power. And it's true that things changed. That she came to know stillness.

Sometimes there are still faint echoes of that city, and of that love. They call out to her when she is in another country, and she is eating a meal outside at a chequered tablecloth, and the food is all salt and ripeness and the night is rushing towards her, and if she still drank she would be two glasses down, and the world prickling, awake, but eventually she had to leave that behind too. Or when she is looking out over a long, cold sea. When she is winding through a street of tall, stucco buildings, or sees a red carnation. These echoes feel like a twinge from a healed bone, the way it still aches sometimes, when you least suspect it.

Second room, third. She skirts the space, doesn't want to reach the painting too quickly. Footsteps, her own and those of others. Still the old superstition, the love of a ritual, something to keep the fabric of a specific universe whole and safe. Nobody notices her. Nobody follows her.

She sits on one of the sofas, upholstered in satin, and waits for a moment. Breathes, for a moment. Takes stock of herself, of how he might see her. Hair shorter, sleeker, boots of shining leather, creases at her eyes. Would he follow her today, if he were to see her for the first time? She doesn't know. She is no longer a girl, formless and tender-hearted. She still can't bring herself to throw away the faded dress she was wearing when he first touched her, as if that girl still lives within it.

After Clara returned from the city of impermanence, she left the real one for a while. A different city seemed a fair counterpoint, a place of dailiness that belonged neither to her nor to him. But she still went to the perfume counter at the airport on her way and sprayed his cologne on the paper tabs, and then she wept, because all her things would smell of him.

The foreign city was on the shores of a beach, and in the early morning she swam, and in the evenings she drank steadily in bars, or alone in her room which did not overlook the water. Everything seemed flat, even starry skies, even sun-warmed seas, but she tried to make for herself a new belief, which was that life would not always feel unbearable. She had to attend to this belief with the single-mindedness she had shown to the previous ones underpinning her world.

Perhaps he is in the city of impermanence again, with another. She thinks about this sometimes, and wonders what it might look like for him. She pictures the cold water replaced by verdant grassland. Pictures a woman, fair-haired, walking out into wild flowers. Together the woman and Francis lie on a bed not dissimilar to theirs. But Clara cannot picture her face; she cannot place whatever she might be to him.

There are still days where she thinks that, if she could have just one hour in the city of impermanence, she would do anything. She would pay any price to wake with Francis into shimmering light, the square brimming with music, the untethering from the world. She didn't realize she had been searching for such untethering. In some ways, she understands, she will always be searching.

Finally, Clara enters the room where the painting is displayed. There is no painting she knows better in the world, no painting she has spent longer standing in front of, taking in each detail, and yet she remains unsure of its true meaning. But it is the thing that lasts, if anything lasts. She has thrown out the bloodstained socks, used the soap, discarded or lost the cardboard tabs, the key card, the scraps of paper. All the other objects have slipped into dust, and Francis may be in this city or elsewhere, and nobody will know what she meant to him, and any accounts of their time there can only ever be an imperfect rendering. For a moment she sees Francis, standing to her right, and she feels the echo of her body calling to his, she feels the remnants of the elastic, just threads now, that still linger, but the man turns and it is not him. The man, the stranger, senses her eyes on him, and looks up. He fixes his gaze. Clara turns away. She moves to the next room.

And there they are; she sees the backs of them. Arturo, his partner, a toddler holding a balloon who is their daughter. Another man, two women. Clara walks quietly, trying to surprise them. But they are expecting her. The child turns around first, runs to her. Only a little unsteady. The third man, not a stranger and not Francis, turns around too, gets to his feet. He walks to her, puts his hand lightly on her arm. Hello, he says. We've been waiting for you.

Arturo and the others follow. Clara takes the balloon. Shared object, shared life, shared endeavour. The small crowd of them, together, in beauty's light-filled room.

Acknowledgements

It's an unbelievable honour to be publishing my fourth (fourth!) novel, and I'm so grateful to everyone who has brought *Permanence* into life. Thank you for ever to my agent, Harriet Moore, who helped me see what this book could be in its earliest stages and encouraged me to be as weird as I needed. Thank you to Gráinne Fox, for steering it fabulously on its way in the US. Thank you, again, to my genius editors Hermione Thompson at Hamish Hamilton and Margo Shickmanter at Avid Reader Press – it's been such a rare and glorious privilege to work with you both continuously throughout my career, and I am for ever so grateful for your wise and rigorous edits and thoughts. Thank you to everyone who brought this book into being, especially Simon Prosser, Ruby Fatimilehin, Laura Dermody, Caroline Pretty and Ellie Smith in the UK, and Rhina Garcia and Caroline McGregor in the US.

I wrote big chunks of various drafts of *Permanence* in the spare rooms of Emmie Francis in Peckham and Carys Owen in Neukölln – both beautiful spaces and times of focus that I will always be thankful for. Thank you, thank you, Emmie and Carys. A lot of it was also written and edited in my local library on the Lea Bridge Road, so a thank you to Waltham Forest Council too (and please support your libraries!). Thank you to the British Council for a trip to the Ceylon and Kerala literary festivals, where I got a lot of editing done and was reinvigorated by many brilliant conversations on writing. And thank you to the UNESCO Prague City of Literature residency, where I wrote the very first scraps of what would become this novel.

Thank you to all of my friends and family for love, support, and conversations about love and writing and the world, with an extra-special mention to Ed John, Nia Davies, Krista Williams, Jess Rochman, Lauren and Jake Salmonsmith, Beverley Murrow, Sarah Gado, Lucia Osborne-Crowley, Elisha Hartwig and Maria Dimitrova. Thank you to my parents, Martin and Caerie, and to my sister and brother-in-law, Annys and David Rudman. And an extra-special thank you to Luke Bell, for caring for me and encouraging me in so many ways.

The conversation on page 228 contains an echo of Raymond Carver's 'Rain', one of my favourite poems, published by Vintage in the 1996 collection *All of Us: The Collected Poems*.